# AFRO NERD IN LOVE

© 2013, 2019 Randolph Walker, Jr.

Image used courtesy of Saulius Rozanas

10 9 8 7 6 5 4 3

ISBN 9781020001062

45 Alternate Press, LLC
Hampton, Virginia

# AFRO NERD IN LOVE

## A NOVELLA

### RAN WALKER

*For Riva, Nsayel, Van, and Kat*

*It's time.*

*Afro Nerd* (*n.*) – an African American with diverse cultural influences, usually identified as a member of the New Black Aesthetic or Post-Blackness; also more commonly referred to as a "blerd" or black nerd.

*Women are made to be loved, not understood.*

*~ Oscar Wilde*

## RED BEANS AND RICE

There's nothing like a wedding to make you feel lonely. You would think the drive from a metropolis like Atlanta to the boondocks of Daily, Mississippi, by yourself would be a lonely enough experience, but it pales against the atmosphere of young love at its apex, on full display, in glorious celebration. When black people gush over "black love," I wonder if it's because they're proud of seeing two people happy and in love or if they are actually jealous they don't have the same thing. Don't get me wrong: I'm proud of Dizzy and Lailah for taking the leap, but after we finish doing the electric slide, I'll be driving five hours back to my one-bedroom apartment outside of Atlanta, where I will be, you guessed it, alone.

I'm in the middle of the sixth CD of my Walter Mosley audiobook when I pull up to the Daily Inn, a two floor motel that looks like it used to be a motel from another chain. I check into my room at the end of the first floor and prepare to take a quick shower. I don't have to be anywhere for at least four hours, so I figure I will drive around this small town and see what there is to do here. After all, small towns in Mississippi tend to have quite a bit of history to them, if you were to believe William Faulkner.

Just as I'm about to hop in the shower, my cell phone rings. I glance at the screen display. It's Julian.

"J?"

"What's up, Chucky? You here yet?"

"I just checked into my room. I was about to grab a shower."

"No time for a shower, man. I need your help with something, so get your ass over here."

"Where are you?" I ask, unsure if I would know the location, even if he told me.

"I'm downtown across the street from the park."

"Where is the park?"

"Chucky, this place is so small you can't miss it. Just go to the main drag you passed when you went to the motel. Bust a left and drive down about a mile. You can park pretty much anywhere. I'll be at the park by the gazebo."

"Is everything okay? Do I need to bring anything?"

"Dude, it's not life or death. Just get down here. I need your help with something."

"All right. I'm on my way."

When I hang up the phone, I sigh. I haven't even been in this town a good ten minutes and my friend J is already putting me to work.

---

J WAS RIGHT. I HAD NO PROBLEM FINDING THE PARK.

Interestingly, the park takes up the entire block, and when I look across the street, it appears that the park continues on for several blocks, breaking only at the streets that intersect the park's walking trail.

"Damn, Chucky Buckner!" J says, as I step from my car. "You look like you done lost half of yourself. You look good, dude."

"Thanks, J," I respond, dapping him and giving him a hug.

I haven't seen J in roughly four years, but we have been keeping in contact over Facebook, and I know he's having some new success with his record store in Harlem. Of course, he looks just like his Facebook avatar, but I haven't used a current picture since I finished grad school, back when I was topping out at three hundred pounds.

"How did you lose it?" J asks, swiping his hand down my now flat stomach.

People love to ask that question, as if the answer will unlock the secrets to the universe. J, however, is still tall and thin, so I know his question is more out of curiosity, not because he is planning to implement any of the things I say.

"Just controlling my portions and exercising more."

"That's it? No Slimfast or Weight Watchers?"

"No. Just eating better. You know what they say, 'Burn more calories than you take in.' No surprises here."

J nods. "I'm proud of you, Chucky. You look good, dude. Cool is gonna flip out when he sees you."

"How's he been doing?"

"Cool looks like he'll be the next one headed to that altar. He's on Denise like a fly on a fresh mound of shit." Looking around, J adds, "Man, it looks like you and me are the only ones still on the market. Who would have thought that Dizzy would be taking the plunge—and with Lailah? Definitely didn't see that one coming."

"Yeah. I knew he always dug her back when we were in college, but I just thought it was a phase. Glad to see that they're of the same accord now."

J pats my stomach again and smiles. "That fuckin' Chucky Buckner! Boy, you need to keep up whatever you're doing. That diesel look is working for you."

"Thanks."

I look around the park and see a handful of people having late lunches, and that's when it hits me that I still haven't eaten anything since I left the apartment this morning. I have a protein bar in the car that I can eat when I finish up here with J, and that will have to carry me over until I can get a lay of the land with regard to my restaurant options.

"So Chuck, here's the deal," J starts. "Akil, the best man, was supposed to be coordinating with me about these strippers, and everything was supposed to be on point with that, but I just got a buzz from him not too long ago about the fact that things he set up in Memphis fell through. So no women for the bachelor party tonight, know what I'm sayin'?"

I nod, still clueless as to how I factor into any of this.

"In fact Akil is out there right now trying to make a miracle happen and round up some strippers from somewhere more local, but this town is too conservative for that kind of shit. Hell, the county is dry with not a fucking drop to drink for at least thirty miles."

"Okay. So what do you want me to do?" I figure that I may as well put it out there, since he clearly had an agenda when he called me. He could have easily waited until the rehearsal to catch up with me if it was just about that.

"I want you to help me get this bachelor party together. The way I see it, the more heads we put together, the better chances we'll have of pulling this thing off."

I don't mean to laugh, but it comes out anyway. "What makes you think I know anything about bachelor parties? I've never even been to one. You guys used to call me the 40-year-old virgin, and you think I know about rounding up some strippers? J, you're giving me way too much credit. Seriously."

J shrugs. "Maybe. Maybe not. I always figured you to be the smartest one out of the crew, with your 97th percentile on the SAT and all."

"That's book knowledge. I know next to nothing about dealing with women outside of what Maya and I had for roughly three months."

"Then the B-Side kicked in, huh?"

"The what?" I ask.

"The B-Side. Like how people start showing their true colors after the third month."

"I don't know, man. I just know that things weren't going all that well, and—well, I don't know. Maybe she just found me too boring or something."

"Were you hittin' it?"

"Yes." I am embarrassed that I am blushing. This is the first time that I have admitted to anyone that I lost my virginity. And while it took me a little time to figure out how to get Maya off, I have no illusions that I'm all that good a lover.

"Well, I'm looking at you now, and you look like you would have no problem pulling a female. So that makes you even more useful than I thought you would be in the first place," J says.

I don't know whether to feel complimented or dissed.

"So what do you want me to do?" I finally ask.

"I hear there's a university in the next town over. Go on the yard and ask some of the brothas what's up. Ask any of the Greeks. They tend to know that type of shit."

"Then what? Call you and give you the info?"

"Yeah. That'll work," J says.

J daps me and is on his way. I walk back to the car, open my protein bar and wonder how J managed to get me to go along with this craziness. I feel too old to be chasing down strippers, and I feel even more awkward approaching people I don't know to get this kind of information. Before I get too anxious, I take a bite of the bar. It's not all that delicious, but it's sustenance.

There's a part of me that thinks I need to do this kind of thing, though. It's important for me to get out of my shell and have adventures. I don't want to always be the squarest dude in the room. Maybe this whole trip could be the adventure that I need so I can have my own story when the fellas get together and start swapping them.

I plug in my GPS and head toward the university, my stomach already filling with bubbles.

———

ONCE I FIND PARKING THAT'S NOT DESIGNATED FOR

students and faculty, I walk over to the building that reads "Student Union." The interior is so swanky that I feel as though I'm stepping into a mall. The food court would put the one at my alma mater, Ellison-Wright College, to shame. Not only do they have all of the traditional fast food chains, but they have a vegan spot, too. The line to the Starbucks is so long that one would think it was the registration line at a historically black college back in the days before the Internet.

Because it's early afternoon, the union is bubbling over with students eager to get a pick-me-up for their afternoon classes or students celebrating because they had the good sense to get all of their classes out of the way in the morning. I spot a few fraternity guys over by one of the booths toward the back of the union. Even though I'm at least ten years older than they are, I still feel like I'm somehow seeking their approval. When I was at Ellison-Wright, I didn't even think about trying to pledge. It's not that I wasn't fascinated by what they did and how they appeared on the yard; I just knew I wouldn't make the line. I didn't have the strength, physical or otherwise. I would have been the guy my whole line hated, the one who always came up short. My mother used to say that she would rather I be Phi Beta Kappa than anything else, and since that was the oldest Greek letter organization in the country and they voted in members based primarily off of cumulative grade point averages and community and school service, I was able to put myself into a good position to get tapped into my school's chapter during my junior year. Still, it wasn't the same as being a member of the National Panhellenic

Council, where you took over lines and did step shows and pulled five times the quota of female attention guaranteed at a small Historically Black College. In short, the guys I see at the back of the union represent everything that I am not—for one reason or another.

I walk slowly toward the booth of guys, trying to figure out how to best bring up the subject of strippers. The more I think about it, the more I am convinced there is no smooth way of doing it. It probably doesn't even matter how I bring up the subject. After all, these guys are Greeks, not geeks.

"Yo," I say, feeling like an old dude trying to sound young. "Y'all know where a brotha can find a stripper. I'm trying to set it out for my boy's bachelor party."

To say the reaction I get from these guys is one of incredulity would be a massive understatement.

"Excuse me," one of the guys says, addressing me as if he is a candidate for a job interview. He's wearing a Greek lettered cardigan sweater and a matching tie. "We're actually discussing a fundraiser for the American Red Cross. Maybe when we're finished one of my brothers can assist you, but right now we're handling business."

I feel like such a loser, the odd man out once again. In all of the years since I was in college, I still feel like I don't belong.

"My bad. It's just an emergency, that's all. I just drove from Atlanta, and this got tossed on my lap." I have no idea why I am explaining any of this to guys who are just a few years beyond being kids themselves.

As I walk away, I hear somebody behind me call out, "Wait up!"

I turn around and one of the guys from the table trots over to me. "Sorry for my brother over there. He's all business, all the time. You visiting from the ATL?"

"Yes. Just got here. And the first thing they do is hit me with this. So I'm just trying to make the best of a bad situation. That's all."

"Well, check this: I know this guy named Ty, who is a DJ. He knows a lot of people. Let me hit him on his cell phone right quick and see what he can do."

Within a few seconds, this guy has made contact with the DJ, and the DJ has agreed to meet me in half an hour in front of the union to offer his help.

I thank the young guy, and he just nods as if it's all in a day's work.

As the guy walks away, he says, "I hope you guys send your boy off in style."

"Will do," I say, heading toward the front of the building.

---

THE DJ IS RIGHT ON TIME AND GIVES ME A NAME AND a phone number, which I quickly text to J.

By the time I make it back to Daily, J has called to thank me for saving the bachelor party. I tell him, "no problem," but I still feel like I haven't done anything special.

When I get back to my motel room, I take a long, hot shower and prepare for a catnap, when my cell phone rings again. I swear I haven't used my phone for talking this much since I upgraded to the latest model three months ago.

"Chuck? This is Dizzy. You busy?"

"Nope," I lie. "What's up?" I am staring at my bed, thinking of how wonderful it would be to close my eyes for just a few minutes. But this is Dizzy, and he's the main reason I'm here.

"I need you to go over and help out at the church, if you can. They're putting up the flowers and ribbons and all that stuff."

"So you thought of me when you heard about flowers and ribbons. FYI, Diz, I don't have a vagina."

He laughs. "I'm not fucking with you this time, Chuck. There's a little bit of lifting that needs to be done, and Akil and J aren't answering their phones right now. They just need some muscle over there— or whatever you can provide." He laughs again, but I know I'll have the last laugh since he hasn't seen me in a few years, either.

"No problem. I have the address already from the wedding announcement you guys sent out a while back. I'll be there in a few minutes."

I can hear Dizzy exhale. "Thanks, man. I owe you one."

"Negro, don't start counting now. But I got you."

When I hang up the phone, I stare longingly at the bed for a few moments before I lock up my room and head over to the church.

───────

ON THE DRIVE OVER TO THE CHURCH, I CAN'T HELP but think about how much I wish I had a girlfriend, my own Michelle Obama. I wasn't even thinking this way before I met Maya, but after having been in a relationship and having had that frame of reference for what it's like to have someone to hold you and kiss you and love you, it's hard to go back to nothing. The void is so wide that you can't help but try to fill it with other things. For me, it seemed as good a time as any to get my health together and see if I could get myself off of my cholesterol and blood pressure medications. I was even pre-diabetic and sliding down hill before I had a heart-to-heart with my doctor and he told me that I had to do something or I was going to be in pretty bad shape in a few years.

Losing the weight wasn't as hard as I thought it would be, that is as long as I didn't make excuses. I got rid of all of my junk food and replaced it with vegetables and fruit and started counting my calories. I quickly realized that I could still eat a lot of the same foods if my portion sizes were smaller and I shook loose the fried foods and sodas. The doctor challenged me to do at least four hours of exercise a week, so I joined the gym in my neighborhood and started doing a combination of weights and aerobic exercises. Without a woman to go home to, I found that I didn't have much else to do but commit to the program. I went from three hundred pounds to one hundred and eighty in less than nine months, and now it's so much a part of my lifestyle that I couldn't shake it if I tried.

I'm still lonely, but instead of ice cream, I have protein shakes.

The church is large and situated out in the country, so it looks even larger with all of the unpopulated ground around it. I park on the side and go in.

Outside of Dizzy's mother, I have no idea of who any of these other people in the sanctuary are. She immediately comes up to me and hugs me.

"Boy, you have lost a lot of weight!" she says, holding me. "Last time I saw you I couldn't even get my arms around you."

"Thank you, ma'am."

"How's your grandmother doing?"

"She's been a little tired lately, a little under the weather, but she's okay."

"Well, you tell her I asked about her," Mrs. Parker says.

"I will," I respond. "Dizzy told me that you all needed help putting a few things up over here."

"We could definitely use the help."

"Well, I'm at your disposal."

Mrs. Parker ushers me around to a stack of brown cardboard boxes and asks if I could take out the parts and start assembling them. They look like decorations that will be affixed to the pews, and while they are elegant, there's nothing complicated about them. As I begin to plow my way through the boxes, I hear a voice.

"So you're the only guy helping out here? I take it you're the only boy scout in the group."

I look up and am startled by how beautiful this woman is. Her light brown skin glows under the lights of the church, and kissing those wonderfully full lips immediately floods my mind. I fumble for words, but they fail me. Instead, I come across looking like a deer in headlights. A beat passes as she waits for me to say something, and when I don't, she shrugs and says, "Well, okay then," and turns to walk away.

"Hold on," I mumble, not sure what I want to say, but knowing that I need to say something to regain some semblance of "face" here. "You know how it is. A brotha pulls into town and finds himself being put to good use every second he's here."

"Yeah, right," she says, lifting an eyebrow. The subtext is clear: *this Negro is a strange one.*

"I'm Chucky," I say, rising from the boxes and extending my hand to her. I know that I should wait for her to do that, but I'm afraid that the only way for me to touch her hand is if I make the first move.

She grasps my hand lightly. "Marcia. I'm the maid of honor."

"Mar-see-ah," I repeat slowly. "That's a beautiful name," I say, as if my opinion on the matter is actually warranted. "I'm a good friend of Dizzy's. We were roommates in college for a spell."

Marcia nods her approval. "Yeah, Lailah and I met in college, too."

"So you're from Atlanta?" I ask.

"Yeah. I never left."

"Me, too. I can't believe that we have never met. It seems like our paths would've crossed by now since our friends are getting married."

"Well, we're meeting now," she says, slowly stepping away to return to what she was doing before I arrived.

"Maybe we can talk later."

"Yeah, right," she says again. She's indulging me, and I know this, but I am so attracted to her that I don't even mind.

An hour later, as I am finishing up the ornaments and preparing for the rehearsal (and the return of all of the groomsmen who left me hanging), I am still thinking about Marcia, wanting desperately to talk to her again.

---

THE FOLLOWING MORNING, HOURS BEFORE THE wedding, the guys are still talking about the strippers from last night. Between Akil and J, they were able to pull off a night to remember. Three girls showed up and put on shows that rivaled what one might see in an after-hours music video. There was even a stripper who did a trick with pool balls!

Somehow the fact that the bachelor party went off without a hitch was credited to me, and I was being congratulated and patted on the back all night, when all I did was get a phone number. Needless to say, such adoration made me feel much cooler than I knew I was.

Even as we groomsmen line up to take pictures of ourselves wearing the watches that Dizzy bought us, the guys are still talking about how I saved the day. I just shrug my shoulders, knowing that I don't have the courage to do much beyond what I did manage to do and that if it were left to me to actually "round up" the strippers, the guys would have been in "hard leg" city all night, cursing each other out.

The wedding goes according to plan, and I line up with the other groomsmen. My only regret is that I'm not paired with Marcia as we come down the aisle. That distinction is left to Akil, since he's the best man. Still, I can't take my eyes off her. If she looked amazing yesterday, I can't even put into words how she looks today. She is wearing a cranberry colored dress that reveals her shoulders and the top of her back. I notice a small tattoo on her shoulder blade as she walks past me to get to her spot, and the flawless hue of her light brown skin continues to radiate with light. Her hair is pulled into a bun, but I can see those bouncing curls eager to spring back into their natural state when she takes them down.

Throughout most of the ceremony, I try not to stare at Marcia, but it's next to impossible. I should be listening to my boy profess his undying love for his bride, but instead I am trying to concoct a way for Marcia and I to connect once we return to Atlanta. Does she have a man? If she does, wouldn't he be here with her? Did she seem at all interested in me yesterday or I am swimming upstream here? I can't slow my mind down long enough to concentrate on anything. I'm a ball of butterflies and confusion.

Thank God I am able to tune in to the "I do's." It's only then that I see Dizzy's face and know that he's marrying the love of his life. Lailah has tears in her eyes as she kisses him. Both of them smile like lottery winners when they jump the broom, and before I know it, the ceremony is over and we are preparing to shoot the last of the wedding party pictures.

Once the pictures are finished, Akil walks up to me. "Chucky, bruh. I'm not trying to get in your shit, but dude you look a little bit thirsty up in here."

"What do you mean?"

"Dude, you're so obvious. Everyone in here knows you're feeling Marcia. Man, you gotta put your tongue back in your mouth. Have some fucking dignity. If you're gonna get at her, don't look so damn thirsty."

I don't even know how to respond to Akil, but I'm so embarrassed I want to run somewhere and hide. If the wedding party didn't have to be introduced at the reception, I would high-tail it back to the motel and hide my face for the rest of the day.

Instead, I find myself riding in the limousine with the other members of the wedding party, desperately trying not to make eye contact with Marcia, or anyone else for that matter.

---

I READ SOMEWHERE THAT THEY THROW RICE AT NEWLY married couples as a way of wishing them a fruitful union. It's a polite way of saying that you're married now so it's time to get to it and give us some children. I figure I will never have children during this lifetime, regardless of what someone throws at me. (In fact, if they threw rice at me, I'd probably scoop it up, take it home, and boil it up with some red beans.) And while I'm cool with the fact that my bloodline will stop here, I know my grandma isn't. She has always wanted great-grandchildren, even more so after my mother passed away. I can understand that, too. What makes it messed up for me is that because I have my mother's last name, I am the last of this line of Buckners—for whatever that's worth. That means that the Buckner (yes, I *am* that corny) stops with me.

At the reception, I'm no better at concealing my growing interest in Marcia. Now I'm starting to feel like a stalker, which makes me feel even guiltier about looking at her. I'm that creepy guy now, and once a woman thinks of you as either creepy or crazy, you're forever stuck with that monicker.

As the bride and groom make their way around to greet the people at the reception, J walks up to me.

"That fuckin' Chucky Buckner. My man, a hundred grand. Pimp of the universe. What's up with you?"

"I'm good," I say. "Just chillin'."

"That's what's up," he says, looking around before leaning in closer. "Hey, lookahere. You gonna keep holding up the wall or are you gonna step to this girl. Inquiring minds wanna know."

"Why? What's up?"

"You ain't the only one up in this piece wanting to push up on Marcia. People just bowing out gracefully because you hooked the shit up so good last night with the strippers. The brothas are giving you room to make your move, if that's what you're gonna do. If not, niggas about to Deebo that shit, and that'll be all she wrote."

I know that J doesn't mean his comments as a threat, but that's definitely how I take them. In other words, if I don't make my intentions known to Marcia, then some other dude will make a play for her. There's a part of my mind that knows that type of thinking is sexist and that she doesn't belong to any of us, so why should we stake a claim in talking to her? But the other side of my mind is saying that I have to, in the words of Kool and the Gang, "Get my back up off the wall." I don't like feeling pressured to do anything, but I hate the idea of someone else hooking up with Marcia even more.

"Where is she?" I ask, knowing damn well where she is, since I have been checking her out nonstop since we arrived.

"Right over there," J says, nodding his head slyly in her direction.

That's when it occurs to me that the guys might think I'm going to fumble this anyway. They're just trying to respect my feelings before they dive in and do what they were going to do anyway.

"I'm headed over there," I say.

"Hold on," J says. "Look, Chuck. We go way back like Afros and freeze pops, right? So know that I'm coming at you from a place of respect when I say this."

"Okay. What's up?"

"You're a good guy, a good friend. I want to see you do well."

"And?"

"And, well, you don't give yourself enough credit."

"What do you mean?" I say.

"I'm just saying that you've been in the gym gettin' your swole on and buffing up and shit."

"And?"

"And dude, I don't know if you realize that about yourself. You're a different guy now, but I sense you're still walking around here feeling like you're a three hundred pound nigga built like a Hefty bag full of old clothes."

I squint my eyes, not knowing how to take his comment.

"What I'm saying," he continues," is that you still act like you did when you were younger, like you're still getting a handle on your self-esteem."

"Really?" I say, incredulous. "When did you become a psychologist?"

"Yo, I'm coming at you from a place of love, dude. Hold your head up. Be confident. Women respond to that."

I nod my head, trying to conceal my hurt feelings. Maybe he's telling the truth. Maybe I *am* still thinking the same way I would have before I lost the weight. After all, nine months is not a long time to change how you see yourself, not when you've been fat your entire life.

I take a deep breath and walk over to Marcia. She's standing by herself, and when I reach her, she smiles.

"Chucky, right?"

"Yes. Marcia, right?"

She smiles. "I have a question for you."

"What is it?" I ask. I'm a little unnerved by her directness, but I play it cool.

It seems like it takes her forever to speak, but when she opens her mouth, she says simply, "What took you so long to come over here and talk to me?

## 2

## ACTION(LESS) FIGURE

J, Cool, Dizzy, and I were all in school around the same time, although J and Cool went to Morehouse and Dizzy and I went to Ellison-Wright. Because Dizzy and J are cousins, we all formed an inter-campus clique. J was always the wild one, the one most likely to jump first and think later. Cool was the laid back dude, even back when he was just going by his birth name, Chauncey. Dizzy, who ended up being my roommate, was a regular dude, a little on the nerdy side, but suave enough to move around in a lot of different circles that were closed off to me. I was the straight up Afro Nerd. Not only was I heavy, but I kept my hair long, using as an excuse the fact that a woman would take pity on me and want to braid my hair (a sure-fire way to get some female interaction in my stale personal life). Years later, a writer named Junot Díaz wrote a Pulitzer Prize-winning novel called *The Brief Wondrous Life of Oscar Wao*, and I would see myself in the sloth-like, fat Afroed protagonist the moment I started reading the book. I'm so glad I wasn't in school when it came out, because I might've picked up another nickname. Hell, who am I kidding? Only a certain type of person reads literary fiction, and the would-be bullies I was up against were not remotely in that category.

Needless to say, my posse, this "band apart," a la Tarantino, has always had my back, as they do now, and they have converged in my motel room, sans Dizzy (who is enjoying his wedding day) and plus Akil (Dizzy's best man), to tell me how I should proceed now that I have Marcia's phone number.

"Wait at least a week before you call her," J starts.

"A week?" says Akil. "This is not the nineties. If you want to make a move, go ahead and make it off the top."

"Hell," J responds, "waiting a week is still good advice, regardless of how long folks have been doing it. Men aren't supposed to come off as thirsty. Give it some time. Let it breathe."

I shake my head, not because I'm confused as to who is right, but because I have sadly managed to elicit this type of sympathy. Am I really this much of a lost cause that I would merit the posse convening for me in an intervention like this? It's all embarrassing, but I don't want to ruffle any feathers saying anything about it. If they're willing to share their knowledge with me, I'm game. Pride definitely comes in second to knowledge. Even I know that.

"Well, when you do catch up with her, set up a date at a restaurant in the 'hood," J says.

"Man, where are you getting this stuff from?" Akil says to J, before turning to me. "Don't listen to him, Chuck. You want to set a standard on a first date. Let her know you're not some scraggly nigga from the SWATs. Get your Ralph Lauren gear and some 'smell good' and take her out in style. Let her know you're the man."

J shrugs and looks at me with his mouth twisted. "I mean, you can do that and all, but really you don't want to come off as a cardboard cut-out of every other dude in Atlanta. First, you take her to a spot like JR Crickets, a wing joint with a big screen TV that plays the latest sports games. Why wings? Get all of that pretense out of the way. Get her where her thumbs are sticking out from sauce and grease. That way you can cut through the bullshit off the top. Get to know her for who she is now. Don't play those games where people put on shows for each other and realize that they can't stand the other person when the B-Side sets in."

"You really live and die by that shit, don't you? B-Sides and Remixes?" Akil says.

"It's like they say in that old gospel song, it ain't failed me yet."

Listening to these two brothers go back and forth is interesting but unproductive. I am neither of them, so I figure I will have to find my own approach—whatever that is. And that idea totally unnerves me. I don't think I could fake like I was all that, so Akil's suggestions are a bit out of my league. As far as J's advice, I do think there is some merit in being real up front, but that scares me a bit more than I'd care to admit. A year ago I was sitting at a computer in my grandmother's house, chatting with girls online—never in person—and I was feeling pretty comfortable about my life. Then Maya came along and gave me a taste of what it was like to really be with a girl who liked me for me. The problem with having had a girlfriend before is that you know how much effort goes into a relationship, so it's difficult to start from scratch with a new girl when things fell apart so badly with the old one.

"I got this," I say, doing my best to make it sound like I really mean it. "I know how to take it from here."

"All right," J says. "But if you ever want to run something by me, just holler."

"Sure," I say.

Akil smiles and says, "Young Simba, you are now a man."

They leave me alone in the room. For a few minutes I just look around at the beige walls and the 32-inch flat screen on the dresser in front of my king-size bed. I will check out the following morning around 9, looking to head back to Atlanta, but there is so much time to blow in the meantime. J will be flying out later tonight, and Akil mentioned that he was going to hit the road in a few hours, so I will be the only guy still in town.

I'm not the kind of person to be bored from being alone though. If that were the case, I would have jumped off a bridge a long time ago. Instead, I grab my cell phone and start checking for things in the area to do that might still be open in the evening. It isn't until I have the phone in my hand and am about to launch my internet browser that the idea crosses my mind that I should call Marcia, just to see how she's doing. From our short conversation at the reception, I learned that she wouldn't be leaving out until tomorrow either, but my nerves kept me from asking what she had planned for later. A woman with her beauty would definitely already have plans, but maybe she would still take my call.

As I dial the number, I think about what J said and how I should wait a week before making a move. Would calling her right now make me seem a little desperate? I contemplate hanging up the phone, but then she answers.

"Hello?"

"Hey, this is Chucky."

"Hey, Chucky. How's it going?"

"Good, now that I'm talking to you."

She chuckles softly, and I choose to take that as a good sign.

"I was just calling to see what you were up to," I say.

"Nothing. Just sitting here watching reruns of the *Real Housewives of Atlanta*."

"Sounds interesting."

"Not really," she says.

I can't tell if that's an invitation or not, but my heart starts beating hard and fast anyway.

"So, uh," I mumble. "Uh, you're just watching TV then?"

"What's up? You want to hook up tonight?"

Damn. She just put it out there. Like that.

"Sure. Why not?"

My heart is about to burst out of my chest like that thing on *Alien*, and I'm suddenly wondering if I was cool enough in my response or if I should've said something smoother.

"What room are you in?" she asks.

The question catches me off guard. I kind of figured that I would be going to her room. Now I'm rushing around the small space tossing things into bags or drawers while I steady my voice to respond. "116."

"Okay. I'll be over in a few. Any idea of what you'd like to do?"

"I'm working on it," I respond, clueless as to what there is to do in Daily, Mississippi, on a Saturday evening.

When I get off the phone, I am almost in panic mode. "Breathe," I tell myself. "You've been here before. This is not your first time at the big show." I have no idea of what I mean when I say these things, only that I need to say something to calm myself down. For some reason, I jump down on the floor and start doing push-ups. They tend to clear my head. Plus, she might touch me, and if she does, I want to feel firm, not squishy. Damn, I'm overthinking this thing. "Breathe," I say again, this time following my own instructions.

The room is as straight as it's going to be, and now I'm combing through one of my cell phone apps searching for things to do locally. Nothing is coming up in Daily. I refuse to believe there's absolutely nothing to do around here. I know there's a movie theater or a mall or something, but nothing comes up on my Internet search. I even call down to the front desk to check with them about malls or movie theaters.

"None in Daily," an older guy says, his drawl so thick with countrified Confederacy that I know he must be telling the truth. "There's one down in Pueblo, about twenty-five miles down Highway 50."

I can barely figure out my way around Daily, so I'm not trying to drive through the boondocks to get to another small town. What if the car breaks down between points A and B? I don't know anyone around here who could help out. I'm not even sure how long it would take AAA to round up a vehicle to come and get us.

Maybe we can just chill and talk, I think. I fan through the playlists on my cell phone, wondering if she'd like to listen to music.

*Really, Chucky? Really?*

On these microscopic, bass-less, weak-ass speakers?

What am I thinking?

I flip through the fifteen channels on the 32-inch flatscreen and see nothing worth watching. By the time I hear her knocking on the door, I realize I have no clue as to what we can do tonight, save one thing that I would be too petrified to even propose.

---

MARCIA ENTERS THE ROOM, HER MOVEMENTS CASUAL and unfazed, as if she were simply perusing the aisle of a grocery store. Clearly, she is nowhere near as nervous about being around me as I am her.

"All of these rooms must look the same, because mine is about the same size as this one. It's just large enough to turn around in."

"Yeah," I say, desperate to sound as carefree as she appears. "I still haven't used the bathroom in here because I'm afraid I might cop a squat and choke to death."

She laughs, and I sigh a huge relief that my crude first joke has gone over well.

"Right?" she says, her cheeks still holding a smile. "I wonder why Lailah and Dizzy picked this place."

"Price probably."

"Definitely had to be the price."

"Want to sit down?" I ask, pointing to the king-size bed.

"Chucky, you're trying to get me in bed already?" she says. "You got two chairs over here, and you are already trying to go *there?*"

"I just figured the bed might be more comfortable than those raggedy chairs," I say, hoping to cover up my faux pas.

"Chucky, I'm just messing with you."

She sits down on the bed, but I remain standing, not sure if it would be too forward of me to sit next to her.

"I was trying to think of a few things for us to do, but I'm drawing a blank," I say.

"Me, too. From what I hear, this place is pretty dead on a Saturday afternoon."

"Well, are you hungry?"

"I'll probably get there in a few. Still feeling that grilled chicken from the reception."

"Yeah," I say. "I feel you."

"So you're from Atlanta, too?" she asks.

"Yes. I was telling Dizzy that I was surprised that I never met you before."

"Atlanta is big. Lots of black folks there," she jokes. "What do you do?"

"I just got a job at a small publishing company down in Little Five Points. We do graphic novels and stuff like that."

"Really? That's awesome!"

I can't tell if she is humoring me or what. "Awesome?"

"Yeah. I'm a fan of Keith Knight of *The K Chronicles*, Harvey Pekar's *American Splendor*, all that stuff."

"You have to be kidding me, right? You actually know who those dudes are?"

"I've been reading graphic novels ever since I was in high school. I think *Ghost World* is the first book I ever finished."

"So then you've heard of Cool Empire Press? That's where I work."

"Boy, you're campaigning to become my favorite person."

For the first time all day, I feel my shoulders drop and relaxation set in. She's a fellow nerd. I can't believe my luck!

"You should come by the office. I can show you around, let you see how we put things together," I offer.

"Are you like an artist or editor or inker or something?"

"Well, I'm an editorial assistant. I started temping there a while back and they brought me on full-time."

"That has to be the coolest job in the world."

"I'm sorry," I say, "but I wouldn't have taken you for a fangirl. You are pretty hot to be a citizen of Nerd Central."

She laughs. "Well, thank you. I was thinking the same thing about you."

I furrow my brow wondering how she could have thought that. I wear my Afro Nerdiness on my damn sleeve. But then I remember that I'm no longer the same Chucky Buckner who was 300 pounds and out of breath every time he walked up the basement steps to his grandmother's kitchen.

"You don't catch brothas who look like *you* getting on the fanboy tip," she adds.

"Well, I didn't always look like this. I used to be 300 pounds, but I started losing it about nine months ago."

"Really?"

As she listens attentively, I tell her about what my life was like before I lost the weight, and against what should have been my better judgment, I mention Maya, although none of what I say fazes Marcia in the slightest.

Then she tells me about the last relationship she was in, which, interestingly, was even farther back than my relationship with Maya. For the next two hours we laugh and joke with each other, and by the time the pizza we ordered has arrived, I feel like I have known her for years, and not just these past two days.

I'm not even nervous anymore. It's not that I'm no longer susceptible to her beauty—because I am— but it's more like I have come to accept her beauty as being complementary to her personality. It feels as though we are kindred spirits, and I find myself wishing the day would never end.

Roughly an hour and half after we finish eating pizza, with Marcia stretched across my bed, barefoot and in her khaki shorts and t-shirt, she asks me, "Who was your first crush? Like celebrity crush."

"I'm embarrassed to say."

"Come on. It can't be worse than mine."

"Who was yours?" I ask.

"No. You first!"

"Promise you won't judge me."

"Only if *you* don't judge *me*," she responds.

I wait a beat before opening my mouth. "It was Carrie Fischer in *Return of the Jedi*. Princess Leia was the sexiest thing I had ever seen. She looked so good in the metal bikini that I couldn't stop thinking about her for months."

"Not bad," she says. "I could see guys crushing on her. Mine is much worse, though. I had a crush on Michael J. Fox, especially in *Back to the Future*."

"Interesting choice. I don't know why I thought you'd say Billy Dee Williams as Lando Calrissian."

"He was old enough to be my dad! There was no way I was going for that," she says, laughing.

"So if I put on a sleeveless goose down jacket, some worn out jeans, and a pair of Nikes, you'd think I was sexy."

"Maybe."

"Well, then it's settled. I'm hitting up Burlington Coat Factory as soon as I get back to the ATL."

She laughs and touches my chest with her hand playfully. It's the first time she has touched me since she's entered the room. And I like it.

"Want to hear something crazy?" she asks.

"Sure."

"I'm wearing my Princess Leia underwear right now."

"You're kidding me. No one has those."

"I don't mean the actual bikini she was wearing, but my bra and panties look like the bikini, at least design-wise. They're brown and intricate. I call them my Princess Leia's."

No sooner than the words leave her mouth, I feel the flapping of butterflies growing in my stomach. They swoop down fast and furiously, and for a moment I stare at her, trying to imagine her dressed in the Jabba slave suit that had fed my imagination through my many years of self-gratification.

"You expect me to believe you without proof?" I ask, in a desperate attempt to satiate my curiosity as calmly as I can.

"Don't challenge me," Marcia responds coyly. "I'm comfortable with my body."

I want to respond, "I want to be comfortable with your body, too," but I shrug instead, letting her know that talk is cheap.

She hops up from the bed and takes off her t-shirt so quickly that I want to beg her to slow down and tease me a bit more. Before I know it, her t-shirt is lying across the bed and she is unbuttoning her shorts. That movement, too, is fast, and her shorts hit the floor in half a second, the khaki crinkling into a light pile. She scoops the shorts with her foot and kicks them onto the bed. It's only when she puts her foot down and places her fists on her hips, like a superhero, that I really get a chance to take in the complete view.

Her light brown complexion looks as if it has been completely moisturized in cocoa butter since she was a baby. Not a lick of ash on her anywhere (I'm just saying, because I've seen a few ashy women in my day). Everything about her is sweet and feminine, from her feet, which look like they have never needed a pedicure a day in her life, to her neck, which clearly never saw the activator of a Jheri curl. She looks flawless. Perfect. Her hips are sweetly curved and her breasts are full and round. Her navel is pierced, emphasizing the flatness of her stomach. All I can do is stare for a moment, trying my best to maintain what I hope is a cool facade.

"You look pretty sexy," I manage.

When I finally notice the design of her underwear, I feel my johnson snap to attention like it just entered basic training. She was right! They do look like Princess Leia's bikini. Years of fantasies come rushing back to my head, and when they collide in this beautiful brown form in front of me, I find that I have to shift to adjust myself.

"Do you think they look like the ones from *Return of the Jedi?*"

"Oh yes!"

"So you like them then?"

I nod so furiously that I fear I might snap my damn neck.

She reaches for her t-shirt on the bed.

"Hold on," I say, pulling the t-shirt away from her.

She smiles in response. "What?"

"I just want to look at you. It's like Eddie Murphy said in that movie *Life*. 'Why fo can't I just sit here and look at yo ass?'"

She laughs and does a little dance in a circle that allows me to see the complete dimensions of her body for the first time. I am now rock hard, like Medusa sneaked a peak of my joint. I feel like I can bang my shit against a windshield and crack it all the way through.

"See?" she says, feigning model poses, clearly comfortable in her skin.

Again she reaches for her t-shirt, but I pull it away a second time.

"What?" she asks, the exasperation in her voice very contrived. "Why do you keep moving my shirt?"

"I don't know. I guess I like looking at you like this."

"You guess?"

"I could look at you like this all day long. For real."

"So you want me to sit around in my underwear?"

"If I had my way, I would definitely want that," I say, smiling, but deep in my stomach, I am more nervous than a long-tailed cat in a room full of rocking chairs.

"What about you?" she asks. "Why should I be the only one sitting around in underwear? Go ahead, Magic Mike. Come up out those clothes."

This is the first time that a woman has ever—in my life—requested that I take off my clothes, and I'm even more excited than I was a few seconds ago. I want to comply with her request, if only to make her happy, but then I can't ignore the fact that I am sporting an erection you could pitch a tent on.

"I would," I start, "but I'm having some technical difficulties."

"Technical how?"

I lean forward putting my elbows on my knees. She sees this and laughs, not in a bad way, but in an amused way.

"I won't judge you."

"You don't understand. I need to wait a few minutes before I take my pants off. You know, it would help if you talked about something else, like your favorite book or something like that."

She laughs again and sits down on the bed beside me. For a second, I fear that she might reach over and grab me—which I pray she won't do, because I'm too excited right now and don't want to pull a Moby Dick (thar she blows!)—but she doesn't.

"I like Tayari Jones, Junot Díaz, Zadie Smith, Victor LaValle, Tananarive Due. You know? Writers who are doing something other than street stuff. I don't know if I have a favorite book though."

"Yeah. I feel you," I say, but in actuality I am trying to remember the starting line-up for the last three NBA World Champion teams (my trick for calming myself down when I get too aroused).

She looks at me for a moment, the silence of the room filling the void between us.

"Maybe I should put my clothes back on," she offers.

"I really don't want you to do that."

"Well, find a way to even the odds then."

I point to the light switch on the wall. "Could you please turn off the lights?"

She stands up and turns them off, tugging gently at the already closed blinds to ensure that they remain closed. Now I can hardly see her, which is perfect, because then she won't be able to see me either.

"Is that better?" she asks.

This is all new territory for me. I'm already starting to feel embarrassed for acting like a little kid with the lights and all, but with Maya, things were slow and glacier-like, in terms of speed. Now, it feels like Marcia and I are about to start whatever this is with a bang. That's definitely a first—and it's a hell of a lot more pressure than I ever thought I would have in a situation like this. I don't even know what to say right now, but I hear an affirmative hum buzz behind my sealed lips.

I stand up and remove my shirt, feeling blanketed by the darkness around me.

"Your silhouette is kickin'," Marcia says.

"Oh. Thanks," I mumble, not realizing that she could make me out in the dark.

I angle my body away before removing my pants. I'm starting to calm down a little, until I feel her hands touch my shoulders.

"You don't have to be nervous around me. I like you. It's cool."

My pants hit the floor and I turn my head slightly. "I know you might not believe me, but I'm not all that smooth with this kind of thing."

"Don't worry about it. Most brothers have *too* much experience with women."

"Well, that's definitely not me," I say, still angling my erection away from her, although, in all likelihood, she can't really see me that well anyway.

"We don't have to do anything that you don't feel comfortable with," she says, and I swear she sounds like a dude when she says this. "Keep in mind, the moment you tell me to put on my clothes, then we can turn the lights back on."

This is intended as a joke, but I can only get out half a giggle before I decide to just turn around and go for it.

I don't know what I expected before our lips touched, but it is nothing compared to the softness that I feel now. I've never been kissed like this— which isn't saying a lot—but it feels like this is the first time a woman has actually desired me. And the feeling is amazing!

"I want you," she says softly, her breath tickling my ear between light touches of her tongue.

I lose myself, and for the moment, I am not Charles Buckner. I am the passion of a Marvin Gaye vocal; I am the embodiment of every note, every melody, every lyric to every great love song ever written.

As my fingers massage the soft skin of her back, I moan in return, "I want you, too."

---

WE LIE IN A WARM, DAMP EMBRACE, AND I CAN STILL feel my body tingling, remembering the feeling of her legs wrapped around my waist. Even with her naked backside now spooned against me, I can feel the phantom movements of her warmth stroking up and down my shaft. I kiss her shoulder blades and she moans softly.

"That was incredible," I whisper into the nape of her neck.

She reaches back and takes my johnson in her hand and begins to massage me back to full erection. Once she is satisfied that I am aroused enough, she turns over and rolls on top of me, straddling me.

"Round two?" I ask.

"Chucky," she says, placing a finger to my lips, sealing them. "I want you to fuck the shit out of me, but don't say a single word. Just do it."

Every word I consider saying stops at the back of my throat. I have never had someone tell me to shut up and fuck them. I am too aroused to be taken aback.

When she eases her soaking wetness down onto me and proceeds to bounce up and down, I am quickly reminded of a person trying to jump up and down on a balloon to pop it. This time, though, I am the balloon.

I widen my legs, lift my hips, and prop her up on

my thighs. She lowers her breasts onto my chest and I scoop my arms under and around her shoulders. With the soles of my feet pressed firmly into the mattress, I start pumping her with the same ferocity she had just given me.

"Ooh, Chucky!" she says, squeezing my arms and feeling my biceps. "Tear it up!"

I move faster and faster, as if I have a battery pack strapped to my back, energizing my hips to move as rhythmically as possible.

"Ooh, this is some good dick!" she says, her words staccato gasps.

I moan my affirmation, careful not to speak.

I slide my hands down her back, feeling the light perspiration of her skin beneath my fingertips. I bring my hands to rest on her ass and grip it firmly, rocking her up and down on me. For a moment I almost feel like a porn star, like I actually have some skills.

As her breasts slide up and down my chest, the hot wetness of sweat and sex makes it feel like our entire bodies are engaged, cell for cell.

She continues talking shit to me, and I feel as though I am going to explode and turn into a glowing ball of energy. I try desperately to remember the names of every player on the championship starting lineups of the past few NBA seasons, one by one. When I see that's not working well, I go to the players on the bench. As I search the pine, she rides my own.

I slow down the movement of my hips in an attempt to calm down, but this only encourages her. She begins to rock against me quickly.

"Right there! Ooh, right there!" she says, her hips rocking back and forth with rabbit-like speed.

As I try to dissociate my mind from how good it feels, I find myself unable to focus. My body is failing me. I want to scream out, but I bite my lip.

"Oh shit!" she says, her body convulsing, as she tries to rise from my chest but staggers and falls against me. Her body contorts and spasms against mine for a few seconds, as she exhales heavily in an effort to catch her breath.

I open my mouth and start to speak, but I find that I can't because I am cumming so hard that the nerves on the sides of my face feel like they are pulling the skin to the back of my skull. Marcia senses this and holds me tightly in an embrace, while pushing herself onto me as hard as she can.

My eyes close and I sigh. My heart is beating rapidly, our sweaty chests continuing to slide against the other. When she finally rolls over to my side, neither of us is able to speak for a moment.

I feel the air conditioning sweep lightly over my chest, and I take in a deep breath. Admittedly, my limited sexual experiences with Maya did little to prepare me for what Marcia just did to me. Although the poet in me would love to call it lovemaking, deep down, I know that I have just been *fucked*. And the shit was good! Now I see why people make the distinction. Making love is more about feelings and mood, but fucking is pure carnal desire, unbridled. I imagine that as long as there are people in the world, there will definitely be a need for both.

"Chucky?"

"Yes."

"Boy, you put it down! Ooh, shit, my legs are still buzzing."

I smile. "I've never experienced anything that intense."

She leans over and quickly kisses my lips before rising from the bed. I try to look at her as she walks toward the bathroom, but I don't have enough energy to lift my body from its current state. I feel as though I just finished running eight miles uphill, but the tingle is still there, that part of her that only moments ago meshed into my body so effortlessly.

Lying alone in the bed, I am dumbfounded by the entire situation. When I got out of bed this morning, Marcia was a simple fantasy; now she is my reality. I begin to wonder what will happen next. Do I ask her to be my girl? I don't know how this thing works. This is what makes having so little experience with relationships so awkward. I quickly make a deal with myself that I will be patient and ride with the flow. When I think about how patient Dizzy was with Lailah (30 years to get to the point that they could be together romantically), I realize that I should treat time as my friend, not my enemy.

Through the bathroom door I can vaguely hear the sounds of the shower starting. Then the door opens, and I see Marcia leaning in the open doorway, smiling.

"You coming in or do you need a formal invitation?"

I smile and rise to my feet.

She extends her hand to me, and I notice its subtle beauty for the first time, those slender fingers and polish-free nails. Her skin looks softer than soft, as if I could swim in the pool of her and lose myself in the tides of her passion.

I follow her into the tub, pulling the shower curtain closed behind us. The hot water sprays down between us like a July storm, and she places her soap-filled hands against my chest. They slide smoothly down my body, and I lean forward, kissing her, the warmth of her lips and tongue making me feel as though my entire body is osmotic.

"This has been nice," she says.

"This is only the beginning," I respond.

She smiles and I see her lips begin to move, but then they stop.

"What's wrong?" I ask.

She shakes her head. "Nothing. Let's just enjoy right here and right now."

I start to speak, but she places her finger to my lips again.

"Right here and right now," she repeats, a weak smile spreading across her face. She continues to rub her hands across my chest, soaping me up.

I nod, although I am now starting to feel the strangest of sensations: doubt.

## 3

## FLYING UPSIDE DOWN

On the five-hour drive back to the Atlanta metro area, Marcia and I trail each other in our respective cars, stopping occasionally along the way to eat or walk around at a rest area. The feeling of her body against mine is still fresh, very fresh, and I feel as though I can't get enough of being around her. I hate that we are in different cars, but we have maintained a constant cell phone conversation the entire time.

When we reach her house, I help her unload her car, but just as we get to the front door, she stops and faces me, her face suddenly unsure.

"Chucky, there's something I have to tell you."

The doubt from last night resurfaces so quickly that I can feel my heart throbbing in my stomach. "Okay."

"I don't really know how else to say this, but I have a boyfriend."

I shake my head, disoriented by her words. "What does that mean? I mean, we spent all last night and today together. I don't get it. How do you have a boyfriend?" I'm not sure if any of these questions even make sense, but in my mind they make about as much sense as what she has just told me.

"It's complicated."

"Complicated how?"

"Have a seat," she says, pointing to the couch in her den.

"I don't feel like sitting down," I say.

"Please," she says resignedly.

She walks over and sits next to me, so I lower myself onto the couch.

"I really like you," I say.

"I really like you, too."

"How can you really like me when you have a boyfriend?"

"That's why it's so complicated."

I shake my head. "At least try to explain all of this to me. You have me kind of out there right now. The least you can do is help me get back to shore."

She nods and takes a deep breath. "Have you ever heard of a Rumspringa?"

"Are you talking about when Amish teens go out to experience the real world before coming back to the community?"

She nods again.

"Are you Amish?"

"No."

"So what does that have to do with anything?" I ask.

She sighs. "I have been with my boyfriend for the past fifteen years, ever since high school." She shifts uncomfortably in her seat, reaching for the best words. "He's the only man that I have ever been with —up until you."

I nod, encouraging her to continue.

"We've been talking about getting married, but we both felt that we needed to sleep with other people before we took that step."

"That doesn't make a lick of sense. Who does that?"

"Please, Chucky. I need you to keep an open mind. I'm telling you something that I've never told anyone, not even Lailah."

"Well, tell me everything. Don't beat around the bush. You owe me at least that much."

"You're right," she says. She sighs again before opening her mouth. "We both decided that if we were going to pledge the rest of our lives to each other, we had to know that we had gotten everything out of our systems. When you've only been with one person in your entire life, there's a lot that you're curious about."

"So I'm a curiosity?"

"No. Well, not entirely."

I stand to leave, but she takes my hand and gently tugs it. "Please sit."

Reluctantly, I take my seat next to her.

"Okay. Well, I have some questions then."

"Fine. Shoot."

"How many men have you been with during this Rumspringa?"

"I already told you. Just you."

"And how long does this thing last?"

"Until the end of this month."

"So just two more weeks then?"

"Yes."

"Then what?" I ask.

"Then my boyfriend and I will get together to find out the next step with our relationship."

This time I'm the one who is sighing. My mind is running so fast it feels as though it's not moving at all. I want to run from this crazy woman, but I am also wanting to be with her again. Even in the oddness of her confession, the irony that we both have only been with one other person sexually is not lost on me. The difference is that this is not my Rumspringa. It's hers.

"Did you enjoy yourself this weekend?" I ask, not knowing what else to say.

"Yes. Did you?"

"Of course. But what did you like about it?"

"You're fun to talk to. You know how to make my body feel good. You're sexy as hell. What else do you want me to say?"

"How did I make you feel—emotionally?"

At this she blushes. "I like you."

"Yeah, you said that earlier. How do you like me?"

She nibbles on her bottom lip and looks away.

"See, the difference between what you're telling me and what I'm feeling for you is this: I want you. And nobody else," I say.

"I want you, too, but it's not really up to me."

"How is it not up to you?"

"I've been with him for fifteen years. He knows me better than anyone else in this world."

"Well, that's only because you haven't given me a chance."

She shakes her head, exasperated, and says to no one in particular, "This wasn't supposed to happen like this."

"What? The sex or the feelings?"

"I don't know anymore."

"Well, your boyfriend is on Rumspringa, too, right?"

She nods.

"So how do you know what he's experiencing?"

"I don't, and I won't."

"How do you know that he isn't catching feelings for someone else, too?"

"I don't know, but I know it wouldn't be fair to him if I did."

"That doesn't make sense, though."

"Chucky, with all due respect, it doesn't really have to make sense to you."

I nod. "You're right."

I look at her as she sits there, and even though she is wearing a perturbed expression, she is still beautiful. I can still imagine the look on her face when she smiles or laughs at my jokes or climaxes atop me. I don't want to give up this easily. Although I am new to all of this, I am quickly beginning to understand the kind of man I am in a situation like this.

"I'll tell you what," I say. "You have two more weeks, right?"

"Yes."

"Spend those next two weeks with me."

"What good would that do?"

"At least you know that you'll enjoy the rest of your Rumspringa. Plus, it's safer to be with just one person during this period. I have only had one other lover in my life, and I'm clean. Plus, I know we get along. You're an Afro Nerd, too. You know this."

She smiles. "I'm not sure that's a good idea."

"Why not?"

"What if I fall deeper for you?"

"Then you won't be alone in that feeling."

She stares at me for a moment, and I cannot tell if she is going to embrace me or kick me out of her place.

"Okay," I say, beginning to feel her slipping away from me. "Let me just ask you one more question."

"Fine."

"Have you done everything that you wanted to do with me? I'd hate for you to leave something on the table if this was just a weekend thing."

"Are you asking me if I'd like to have sex with you again?"

"Well, that's one way of looking at it."

"I don't know. I'm not sure it's a good idea."

This answer throws me off. In the past twenty-four hours we have had sex nine times, and all of them have been spectacular—at least from what I was able to observe. I wonder what J or Akil or Cool or even Dizzy would do in a situation like this. Would they cut their losses? Who cares what they would do, though? I am my own person. The real question is what will *I* do?

"Marcia, follow me on this."

She nods.

I lean over and kiss her gently upon her lips and feel her tongue flutter softly against mine. I place my hand along the side of her face, cupping her jaw as our kiss deepens. I lower my kiss to her neck, and whisper to her, "I am going to make love to you right now. If you don't want this, feel free to stop me."

I keep waiting for her to stop me, but when I finally enter her, I realize that we are both exactly where we want to be.

## 4

# MILLIE JACKSON'S PORCELAIN THRONE

I awake and it's still dark outside. Marcia's head is resting on my chest, rising and falling with each of my breaths. I gently rub her back and kiss her forehead.

She moans and kisses my chest, before lying her head back down and returning to her sleep. For a moment I wonder if she remembers that it's me and not her boyfriend, but I don't stir.

In the darkness of her bedroom, I can hardly make out anything, save the outline of her dresser, a bookshelf, and a desk with a chair parked beneath it. There are picture frames on the dresser, but I can't see them clearly in this darkness. I imagine that they are of her boyfriend, though.

I am lying in her bed, so the notion that she is willing to spend the remaining two weeks with me feels more probable, but what will two weeks do for us? Against fifteen years? Probably nothing. But then again, why does any of this matter to me?

I run the palm of my hand along her bare back, enjoying the smoothness of her skin beneath my touch. This would only matter if I had serious feelings for her. Up until this moment, I have only allowed myself to think of myself as wanting her, but what does that really mean? Wanting her how? To be my girl? To be my sex partner? To love me back?

Hold up. *Back?* Do I love her? I know I'm a newbie on a lot of this stuff, but do I love her? J would probably say that I'm just whipped. Maybe that's it. I'm just a little whipped is all.

But could I love her eventually? *Probably sooner than later.*

I feel her move again. This time, in the stillness of the room, I hear her whisper, "Thank you, Chucky," her head never moving from its place on my chest.

I already know the answer to my question, and it is at that moment that I realize I am willing to give my all and gamble these next two weeks against their fifteen years.

———

"IF WE'RE GOING TO DO THIS, WE'RE GOING TO NEED some guidelines," Marcia says, as she dresses for work.

"Why can't we just go with the flow?"

"Because I need structure. This is already hard enough as it is."

"Okay." I agree only because I don't want her to change her mind altogether. "What are you thinking?"

She turns away from her closet, holding a blouse and a pantsuit. "Well, for one, as much as I love sleeping with you, we can't do that again."

"What do you mean?"

"You'll need to sleep in your own bed, and I will sleep in my own bed."

"Oh," I say, relieved that she meant "sleep" in the literal sense.

"You feel good and all, but I don't want to get used to sleeping with you in this bed."

"Well, let me offer a compromise. How about if you decide you want to sleep with me, then you come to my apartment and stay over there?"

She considers this for a moment. "That's fine, but I probably won't do that either."

"I'm just giving you the option," I say. I notice the picture frames from earlier and am relieved that they are pictures of her by herself.

"Duly noted." She begins buttoning her blouse. "And you have to be monogamous during these two weeks. I have to trust you on this one."

"Not a problem."

"When I say give me space, you have to step back and give me space. Okay?"

I nod. "Fair enough."

"One last thing. And this one is kind of wacky."

"What's that?"

"I want you to make yourself completely and totally sexually available to me whenever I want it. And I need for you to be prepared to roll however I want to roll."

I laugh. "You're serious?"

"Yep. If this is my last chance at something different, I want to go all out."

"Well, I have to ask you something then. Are you into strap-ons, S&M, anal beads, and all that stuff?"

"Damn, Chucky. What kind of freak are you?" she asks, laughing.

"I'm just saying. I'll do my best to follow, but all of that stuff might be a hair outside of my experience level."

"Well, I appreciate your keeping an open mind," she says, "but my desires are a little different. We only have two weeks, so there will be no anal beads." She laughs again. "But if we had another month, maybe."

This time I laugh with her.

"Will I be able to make suggestions for things we can do?" I ask.

"Sure. Why not? Do you have something in mind?"

"I was thinking we could go out to dinner and catch a movie or something."

At this, she bristles a little. "I don't really want to go out in public."

"Don't want to run into him, huh?"

"No. I would rather he not know what I'm doing, and I don't want to know what he's doing, either."

"Fair enough. I can cook dinner then, and we can watch DVDs and Netflix."

"That's fine."

"So why don't you come over tonight, then? There's a movie I'd like for us to watch together."

"Sure," she says, putting on her pants.

I stand and begin to dress. "What type of movies do you like?"

"Interesting question," she says. "I love sci-fi and fantasy, but I also like comedies."

"What kind of comedies? Slapstick? Romantic comedies?"

"I like stupid stuff."

"Like *The Waterboy*?"

"Yep. And I love this movie with Ryan Reynolds called *Waiting*."

"You've gotta be kidding me!"

"You've seen it?"

"Oh, it's so veiny!" I say in my best imitation of the cook from the movie.

"When the girl stands on top of the table and flashes the guys, I almost lose my mind!" she says.

I laugh when I think about it. "So your standards for films are just as low as mine."

"I guess so," she says, putting on her coat. "Well, I have to get to work."

"I should probably do the same," I offer.

She smiles and leans over, kissing me.

I quickly cover my mouth when our lips part. "I know my breath probably smells like gargamel."

"Gargamel? Like the smurfs? Boy, you are crazy."

"Well, what would you say it smelled like then?" I joke.

"If I had to guess, since I didn't get a strong whiff of you," she says, as we prepare to leave the house, "I would say that it probably smells like my pussy."

*Two weeks*, I think, and smile.

## 5

## WALRUS GUMBOOT

Although I have been a notorious foodie most of my adult life, having sampled just about every sumptuous thing my grandmother has ever cooked, I have shifted most of my eating habits to be a bit healthier. I am almost anal with this, too. I guess I suspect that if I ever got hold of a cupcake or cheesecake again, I'd blow back up to well over three hundred pounds. But because I eat a certain way doesn't mean that Marcia does. She probably didn't notice that I only had a single slice of the pizza we ordered over the weekend. If she did notice, she didn't say anything.

I have decided to fix grilled lemon-peppered chicken breast with steamed veggies and a brown rice pilaf. A pot of hot water is on the stove, and a box of gourmet tea bags is on the counter nearby.

By the time Marcia arrives, she confesses to being hungry enough to eat whatever I have prepared. And after complimenting me on my cooking abilities (which I know are meager), she proceeds to clean her plate, but she looks cute doing it (if that's even possible). If she weren't so beautiful, it might be easy to say that she eats like a dude.

"So you liked it?"

"Of course."

"I didn't know if you would be able to get with my cooking."

"Chucky, I loved it because you made it—not to mention it tasted good. I've never had a guy cook for me."

"For real?" I almost ask her about her boyfriend, but I decide it's better to keep him out of this. He's had fifteen years; I only have two weeks.

She sips on her chamomile tea and smiles. "Nerd moment," she announces.

"What?"

"I'm about to have a nerd moment and wanted to give you fair warning."

"No need for that. I'm operating in nerd space all day long."

"Okay," she says. "What are the craziest song lyrics you've ever heard?"

"Sounds like we could easily make a list of those."

"Okay. You go first."

"Let's see. Gotta start with the classic by The Beatles. 'Come Together.' Those lyrics have people scratching their heads all these years later."

She laughs. "What's a mojo filter or a toe-jam football?"

"Your guess is as good as mine. Your turn."

"The Eagles' 'Hotel California.'"

"I read somewhere that they were singing about the music industry," I say. "Up until then, I thought it was a ghost story."

"You probably thought Phil Collins was singing

about seeing a person drown and not doing anything to help him on 'In the Air Tonight,' huh?"

I nod sheepishly. "Who didn't? I don't know if I buy that story about him writing it about his ex-wife."

"Your turn."

"Okay. How about any song by Prince?"

"That's not fair. That's too vague," she says.

I smile. "Well, we could start with looking for purple bananas."

"'Let's Go Crazy,'" she says. "That was an easy one. I thought you were going to go with something like 'Seven' or something like that."

I take a sip of my green tea. "I don't mean to change topics, but I wanted to give you something before it slipped my mind."

"So we're doing gifts now?"

"Well, it's no biggie, but since it wasn't on your list of things from this morning, I felt I could do at least this much."

Marcia twists up her lips like a little kid who is pondering the loophole someone else has discovered in her list. "Just this one time."

"That's fine," I say. "Follow me."

"Where are we going?"

"My bedroom."

She smiles devilishly and hops to her feet. "Let's go."

I am beyond flattered as she takes my hand and eagerly follows me into my room.

"Have a seat on the bed," I say, "and close your eyes."

"Aww sookie sookie now," she says, a smile spreading across her lips as she shuts her eyes.

I reach in my backpack and pull out the gift. "Hold out your hands."

She does as I instruct, and there's a part of me that thinks of setting the books to the side and pulling out my johnson and laying it on her hands. The thought is kind of comical, like Justin Timberlake and Andy Sandburg with their "dick-in-a-box" joke. I know she's probably already thinking that way, just by her earlier reaction. Maybe next time.

I place the books carefully on her outstretched hands. "You can open your eyes."

When she looks down, she laughs in delight. "This is so fucking cool!"

I am relieved as she fans the graphic novels over my bed. She now has all of the graphic novels we have released at Cool Empire over the past year, and by the look on her face, I can tell that I have given her the perfect gift.

"Thank you so much, Chucky. This is really sweet of you."

"I just figured you could see what we've been working on. I also got you this," I say, reaching into my backpack and pulling out a Cool Empire Press t-shirt.

"I am so gonna rock your world tonight!"

"I'm holding you to that," I say.

"Please do," she says, leaning over and kissing me briskly on the lips, before returning to the books, fanning through the stack.

After looking at the gifts for a minute, she moves them to my dresser. She then crawls back onto my bed, tossing her socks and shoes onto the floor. "I want you to put on some music—surprise me—and turn off the lights and lie down with me."

I take my iPhone and scan through some of the songs in my iTunes library, find a track and set it to "genius mix." I place the phone on my speaker dock and hit the light switch. By the time I climb into bed, Mint Condition's "Forever In Your Eyes" is playing softly, blanketing us in the darkness.

"Nice pick," she says, snuggling against me. "I haven't heard this song in years."

I place my arm around her, cuddling her. "I missed you today."

"You did?" She nestles herself into my embrace. "I missed you, too."

"What did you miss about me?" I ask.

"This. You holding me."

I whisper into her ear, "I have been wanting you all day."

"Now you have me. What are you gonna do to me?"

"Whatever you want."

"Well, surprise me."

I rise from the bed. "Close your eyes. I'll be right back."

---

OUR BODIES ARE STILL STICKY WITH THE REMNANTS of whipped cream and chocolate syrup, and the bed is damp from our perspiration. My abs are burning, and I'm still trying to catch my breath. Marcia is stretched out across the covers, the breeze of the ceiling fan sweeping over her beautiful, naked body.

"I want you to spend the night," I say.

"Okay."

I am relieved at the speed of her response. "I'll be right back."

I walk into the bathroom and start a bubble bath, lighting candles and placing them in various corners of the room. When I return to the bedroom, she has not moved an inch.

"Do you think he's doing this with someone right now?" she asks.

The question comes from out of nowhere, and I don't know exactly how to respond. I had convinced myself that she would not talk about him tonight. I was wrong.

"There's no way you would ever know, so there's no point in dwelling on it."

"Maybe."

"Let's try to focus on being here right now, in the present."

She chuckles. "Yeah, but he is probably out there going buckwild."

Resignedly, I ask, "Why do you say that?"

"I don't know. He just seems like the kind of person who would be off the wall if he had the chance."

"Well, let's not worry about what we don't know for sure," I say, offering again to steer the conversation to something more pleasant.

"Chucky, every single time we have been together, you have made me cum. Von never did that."

Von. So that's his name.

While comparisons were inevitable, I was hoping that we could push it off as long as we could. Most of my comparisons between Marcia and Maya were done shortly after the first time she and I were intimate. Then I pushed it all to the back of my head. I have no idea of where any of this is fitting with Marcia's perception of things, though.

"I just want to please you," I respond, filling the silence. I can hear the water running in the adjacent bathroom.

"That's what I like about you," she says. "It's like you want to understand me. When you have been with someone since high school, you change—and they change, too. And sometimes you grow in different directions."

"Do you feel like you might have outgrown Von?"

"That's it. I don't really know."

"Well, you know this doesn't have to just be a Rumspringa. This could be your real life."

She half-chuckles under her breath, as if she is not sure what to make of this idea. I walk back into the bathroom and check the water. When I return, Marcia is sitting on the edge of the bed, her panties in her hands, her leg lifted as if she is about to put them on.

"The water is ready," I offer, extending my hand to her.

She freezes, the fabric of her panties resting around her ankle. She lowers her foot, raising her panties to her knee, and lifts her other foot.

"Don't leave," I say.

"Why should I stay?"

"You're sticky, for one."

She laughs.

"Plus, I want you to stay." I kneel on the floor in front of her, placing my hands on her thighs. "Marcia, this is *our* moment. This is *our* time. I don't want to lose a single minute. Stay with me tonight, and give me the chance to be what you need—if only for this moment."

She looks directly into my eyes, and for the first time tonight I feel like she is really seeing *me*. She inhales deeply. "You're trying to make me fall for you. I can see what you're doing."

I don't respond.

"Chucky, I'm not going to leave him, if that's what you're thinking. This is just our Rumspringa."

I nod. "I understand that. I'm not trying to make you do anything you don't want to do."

"I can't fall in love with you. You have to understand that, and I'm not sure you do."

"I know this is temporary," I respond. My heart sinks in my chest as I admit this.

"I'm beginning to think that this is a mistake, like we might be getting caught up a little bit."

"So you're catching feelings for me then?"

"Shit, Chucky, I don't know."

"Well, don't you owe it to yourself to find out one way or the other?"

"If it were only that easy."

"It can be, if you allow it to be."

She lowers her head, and places her foot down on the floor, her panties still at her knees.

"Walrus gumboot," I say, referencing The Beatles "Come Together."

She smiles.

"Spinal cracker," I add.

"Okay."

"Okay, what?"

"Okay. I'll stay tonight."

"Good. I don't want our bathwater to get cold."

"But Chucky, we have to slow this down some. It's all going so fast."

I nod, but I don't have the slightest clue of how to put on the brakes, and from what she's saying, I can tell that she doesn't either.

## 6

## META-CARE

"Chucky, this isn't going to end well for you," Ran says. "I'm actually surprised that you fell for her this hard. Out of the two million or so women in the Atlanta metro area, you *would* fall for the one you had the least chance of success with."

It's just like Ran Walker to think he can just piss on my parade. I tell you. You work with someone for two years, and all of a sudden they think they know everything about you.

"I'm telling you that something's there. We've been together everyday since the wedding. At first she told me that she didn't want to sleep over, but she's slept over every night this week. I think she's feeling me just as much as I'm feeling her."

Ran smirks. "Is it me, or did you just tell me that she told you what the deal was from jump?"

"Yeah, but I think she's just talking. Trying to save face."

"Or maybe she's letting you know what the real deal is."

"But her actions conflict with what she's saying."

"Think about it," he says. "Is that really the case?"

I spin around slowly in my office chair, taking in my tiny cubicle and then Ran's adjacent space.

"So," I respond, "you're saying that she can make love to me every night and sleep in my bed and watch movies with me and eat dinner with me and it all just be some meaningless stuff?"

Ran shakes his head. "That's not what I'm saying. I'm just suggesting that it might not all be going down in her head the same way it is in yours."

"Damn, you sound like J," I say.

"Who? Your boy in New York?"

"Yeah. That's him."

"Well, I guess great minds think alike."

"Maybe."

I can hear people on their phones in other cubicles and some retro Journey song playing in the background. It's just a usual morning at Cool Empire.

"I hope this works out the way you want it to," he finally says.

I smile. "Well, if I were a character in one of those books you write, how would you make my story end?"

"I don't know, man. I would want you to have a happy ending, I guess. But in all honesty, I have trouble seeing how that could happen when her boyfriend shows up."

I place my index fingers on my temples and rotate them. "I should probably get back to work, man. I figure I'll just take it for what it is."

"Let me know how that works out, though. Seriously, Chuck. I wish you success with this." He scoots his chair back into his cubicle before pushing himself right back and saying, "You ought to take her to Dizzy and Akil's launch party. Let all of the Ellison-Wright folks get a glance at the lady that's straight hijacked your brain."

"I don't know," I say. "We'll have to see."

"A'ight then."

I ease back to my computer. Out of everyone I work with Ran is probably my closest friend. Yeah, he can be brutally honest sometimes, but I can tell he understands a lot of this stuff better than I do and wants to see me in a good space with all of this. I was kind of hoping that he would give me better words of encouragement, though. He was definitely a fan of Maya and me, so I figured he'd be a fan of Marcia and me, too. Maybe he'd change his mind if he ever met her.

I look at the stack of paper on my desk and begin my daily task of sorting things out, making follow up phone calls, sending out letters, preparing for afternoon meetings, and all of the things I do in the day that fall between the lines of my job description. We have a small staff and are between interns, so a few of those duties fall to me, too, since I'm an editorial assistant and pretty much the lowest man on the full-time totem pole.

As I return a few phone calls on my office phone, my cell phone buzzes with a text message from Marcia.

*Plans for lunch?*

I think for a moment, then type, "*No. What's up?*"

A few seconds later I get a response: *Meet me at the corner of Euclid and Moreland at 11:30.*

I stare at my phone. My first thought is that something is wrong and that she can't wait until the end of the work day to call all of this stuff off. My stomach starts to bubble with anxiety. In the seconds that follow I wonder if I should agree to meet her or not. I could be overthinking this, I remind myself.

I punch "OK" into my phone and hit send.

I don't receive any more texts after that one. Instead, I am left to count down the minutes until I leave the office. By 10:30, I am wound pretty tightly, so I roll my chair back to see if Ran is in his cubicle. Thankfully he is.

I explain the text messages to him and ask him his take.

"You know her better than I do. What do you think it's about?" he says.

"I don't know. Part of me thinks that it's something bad."

"Why do you think that?"

I shrug. "Well, she works across town, and she texts me out of the blue asking me to meet her at the corner of Euclid and Moreland."

"So she knows you work in Little Five Points," he says, his intonation flat as he considers this. "Are you sure it was her texting you?"

"What do you mean?"

"You didn't speak to her on the phone—at least you didn't say that you did."

Now I'm starting to get nervous. "No. She just texted me, and I texted her back. Are you thinking that maybe it was her boyfriend texting me from her phone?"

"Hold on, before you get worked up. Have you guys ever texted each other before?"

"A few times."

"What kind of stuff did you text?" he asks.

"You know. Stuff like 'how are you doing' or 'thinking about you.' Stuff like that."

Ran arches his eyebrow, kind of like The Rock, and says, "So you've been putting your feelings into your texts?"

I hadn't really thought of it like that, and I am embarrassed to admit this. I lower my head instead.

"I guess the question you have to ask yourself is if she would have this stuff still on her phone and her boyfriend be around to actually read it."

At this point I am starting to think that I might be on the verge of getting jumped by a jealous boyfriend—or worse. "Shit!" I utter under my breath.

"Chill, Chuck. We don't know for sure. My motto is to not worry until you have something to worry about."

"Is that one of your Zen sayings?" I ask, exasperated.

"Why? Does it sound like one?" he says, laughing.

As the clock ticks slowly to 11:25 a.m., I rise from my desk. I lean over to Ran's cubicle. "Dude, I'm going down to meet her—or whomever."

"Hold on," he says. He types on his keyboard and finishes an email before saying, "I'm rolling down there with you."

"For real?"

"Dude, best case scenario I get to see this woman you're losing your shit over. Worst case scenario, you have backup just in case this guy is on some street shit."

I can't begin to express how relieved I am knowing that someone actually has my back on this. I have managed to scare the hell out of myself with the possibilities of what could happen, but knowing that there's someone who could jump in, if necessary, gives me a reassurance that is hard to put into words. I know I will owe this dude majorly going forward.

We reach the corner right at 11:30 and start looking for anyone walking around suspiciously.

"So you see her?" he asks, looking in each direction.

"Nope."

"Do you know what her boyfriend looks like?"

"Nope."

"Well, just keep your eyes peeled for anything."

I nod, the knot in my throat so hard I can barely swallow.

Then a car pulls up to the curb. It's Marcia behind the wheel.

"It's her," I say, relieved.

Ran cranes his neck to see her. When I open the door and sit down in the passenger seat, he leans in. "I'm Ran. I was just headed to grab lunch and figured I'd wait with my boy until you got here."

"Hi, Ran. I'm Marcia. Thanks for keeping him company." She looks back at the oncoming traffic. "Nice meeting you," she says.

I close the door and roll down my window. "Thanks, dude," I say.

"No problem. By the way, I'll cover for you if you get back late, but don't forget we have a 2 o'clock meeting in the conference room."

I nod. "I owe you one."

He chuckles and turns to walk away.

Marcia leans over and kisses me quickly, and within seconds she is headed toward I-20.

Marcia wastes no time pulling into a multilevel parking deck and driving up to the seventh level and parking in a back corner. During the drive I started to tell her what had crossed my mind before she arrived, but I thought better of it. Instead, I am reflecting on the thing she said when she picked me up: *Remember what you promised me? Any time I need you, you would be available.*

So now here we are, camped out in this parking deck, and I have my seat lowered all the way back. She has crawled into the backseat and is lying low with her legs spread and parted in my direction. As I lie on my side, my shoulder pushed into the cushion of the passenger seat, I lean in and taste her.

"That's it, baby," she says, rocking her pelvis back and forth, brushing against my tongue and then my nose and then my tongue again.

She reaches for my hand and begins sliding in my fingers, as she rubs herself with her free hand.

"Eat that pussy like you want it," she moans, her voice intense and controlled.

I dive in and give it all that I have. My jaws are becoming sore and the awkward position of my body has my side aching, but I'm determined. I want to hear her scream so loudly they can hear her in the ticket booth down on the bottom level of the garage.

Suddenly, I feel her body jerking in stiff staccato movements. "Yes, right there! Right there!" she screams, and then she roars like a lioness and her entire body goes rigid. "Shit! Ooh wee!" She runs her hands back and forth over my hair, as her body begins to slowly relax.

I smile. I don't speak, though. She doesn't like for me to say a lot. She likes me to speak through my body, and I can't tell if that's just a way of her making the moment less personal or if she actually has this preference in general.

"I want you to fuck me good," she finally says.

"Oh, don't worry about that," I respond, my confidence level at an all-time high.

"But not now," she says, easing away from me and pulling up her panties.

"What? Are you serious?"

"Yep. I need to get you back to work. And I have to drive across town."

"That shit can wait," I say. "I'm so hard right now that if I sneezed, I'd cum all over this car."

She laughs. "Then you'll cum hard tonight when I see you."

"You're serious," I say, the intonation in my voice falling. "No reciprocation?"

"Later tonight, Chucky."

"A handjob?"

"Anything you want tonight, it's yours."

I am still sorting this out in my head, when she opens the back door and hops back in the driver's seat. By the time I wrap my mind around what just happened, we are exiting the garage and headed back toward Cool Empire.

"You okay?" she asks when we turn onto Moreland Avenue.

"I'm good," I lie.

"I have always wanted to do that. You just don't know."

I slowly smile. "So that was the first time you

ever did that?" Not that I had ever done that either, but still it is cool that we shared a first together.

"Definitely a first. And the shit was good!"

The male bravado part of me smirks, like "Yeah, I'm a champion!" These words rest just behind my lips, never to be uttered, but, dammit, they are there.

When she drops me off in front of the office building, she leans over and kisses me deeply. "Make sure you drink your electrolytes, because when I get to your house tonight, you're going to need them."

I nod. "Will do."

When I get out of the car, Marcia leans toward me and says, "Chucky?"

"Yeah."

"Thank you. I'm serious, baby. Thank you."

I smile as I close the door.

When she pulls away from the curb, headed back to work, I stand at the front of the building for a second. There are probably a thousand things that could cross my mind: Was it silly for me to worry about her boyfriend? Should I have just rubbed one off in the parking deck to ease the ache in my pants right now? Would next time be even wilder?

I could think about any one of those things. It would only be logical.

Instead, I can only think about one thing: I might have eaten for lunch, but I'm still hungry.

## 7

## JOY IN REPETITION

Marcia arrives just after seven. She is wearing a light cotton dress that hugs every curve of her sexy frame. It rises high on her thighs, and her legs look absolutely amazing. Her heels add an extra *booyah* effect to the entire ensemble. I think back to what Ran said earlier about what a looker Marcia was. If he were to see her now, he'd probably slap me on my back with the pride that only a married man could do for one of his remaining single friends.

"Have you been waiting for me?" she asks coyly.

"You have no idea," I respond.

I have prepared us a light meal, but I am not inclined to touch the food. At least not yet. There's still some unfinished business from earlier.

I take Marcia by her hand and guide her toward my bedroom, where she drops her overnight bag on the floor against the wall. I dim the lights in my room and turn on the lamp by my bed, which I have replaced with a blue light bulb that casts a mellow glow over the room. I start the music on my iTunes playlist and allow the music to fill the room through the speakers on the dock.

I sit on the foot of the bed and lie back, crossing my hands behind my head.

"Strip," I say. "And take your time."

Her eyes grow large for a second as she takes in the authority with which I have delivered my command. "Yes," she responds.

She begins to move her hips slowly, rocking to the beat of the song, which in this case is Zo!'s "Make Love to Me," a sultry ten and a half minute ballad that features the seductive voice of Monica Blaire. Marcia sways sweetly, her right hand gradually working its way to her left shoulder, carefully removing the strap there. She continues moving her body, almost like a belly dancer moving in slow motion, her other strap coming down so that she is able to peel the dress down her body, revealing her smooth skin an inch at a time. Eventually she is standing before me in only her matching turquoise panties and bra, the heels holding together the look in such a way that I am already at full attention.

For a moment, she dances for me, and I feel like I am the most important man in the world. Even in the slow movements of her body, there's an intricacy in each outstretched arm, in each turn of her legs, and in the way that she closes here eyes and dances as if she and I are the only ones in the entire universe.

Her hands ease up her back, unloosening her bra. She catches it quickly, holding it to her chest, her body still rocking to the beat. She opens her eyes and looks directly at me. I smile, and she smiles in return.

Then the bra falls to the floor. Her hands rise to her breasts, taking them tenderly (as I imagine I would) and squeezing them lightly, her fingertips easing to the ends of her nipples.

The smile on my face grows, and my entire body tenses with anticipation.

She then places her hands on either side of her waist, slipping her fingertips beneath the thin lace of her panties. She sweeps her hips even wider, as she eases the fabric down her hips, her thighs, her knees, her calves, and then onto the floor, where she lifts her foot, catching the garment on the heel of her shoe and kicking it softly onto my chest.

Now she stands before me completely naked, save the heels. And she is still dancing.

I am mesmerized by her body in motion. She is a work of art, nothing like those dancers we got for Dizzy's bachelor party. Those were girls who twerked and made it clap for a living. Marcia, on the other hand, is a woman who is focused and content to perform for an audience of one in a way that transcends the possibilities of anything that could occur at a club where men ration out one dollar bills like Wonka's golden tickets.

Marcia is moving like she wants *me*—and me alone. This boyfriend, Von, doesn't exist in this room, in this universe that she is creating for her and me.

"Tell me what you want me to do," she whispers softly, her body still riding the rhythms of the music.

I have been waiting for this request since she dropped me off at work. And I have been going through my mental database of all of the wildest and freakiest desires I could imagine, but all of that goes

out the window now. I just want her—however I can
have her. I respond, my voice a resonant rumble beneath the kicks of the bass drum in the song, "Do
what the song says."

"Yes," she responds, her smile both sweet and de-
liciously wicked. "I will definitely make love to you
with intention and purpose."

She eases me out of my clothing, piece by piece,
kissing me with the revelation of each bare body
part. When she straddles me and takes me in, it is
not the violent fuck of our initial interactions, but
the sweet movement of a woman yielding more than
her flesh to a man. I had imagined that I would talk
serious shit tonight, but I only whisper words of en-
dearment, definitely more Maxwell than Uncle
Luke.

Her body rises and falls over mine, and then my
body rises and falls over hers. We morph into posi-
tions, our movements fluid like water bending
around obstacles, blissfully unaware of any obstruc-
tions. The song repeats and our bodies move in an
interminable passion that is only further enhanced
by my desire to be close to her. The whole of her
body is against mine, and I am taking in this moment for all that it's worth.

I faintly hear the sound of my own voice, as she
looks down on me while I lie on my back. "You are
amazing." It's not an exclamation; it's a revelation.

She begins to moan and she leans over to receive
my waiting embrace. Her arms are wrapped around
me, mine around her, and we are holding on to each
other for dear life, as she moves her hips more
rapidly and forcefully into mine. I feel like I know
her body now, so I feel her when she climaxes in my

arms. But it's not like earlier in the car. This is different.

"Marcia," I whisper, loving the sound of her name as it escapes my lips.

"Love me," she says so softly I wonder if I am mistaken.

I want to ask her to repeat it, but I'm afraid that she won't. I respond, "Yes."

Then she says it again. "Love me."

My heartbeat quickens, and carefully I lift her face to mine. "Say it again," I whisper, nearly breathless.

She looks at me, her eyes focused on me in a way that I have never seen from any woman. "Love me."

At that moment something in me emerges from beyond the artificial wall I have erected in my mind. I can scarcely recognize my own voice, but in the raindrop like electric piano breakdown of song, I distinctly hear the words, "I do love you."

"I love you, too," she responds, lowering her head back to my chest.

I feel tears drip onto my chest, and I hold her more tenderly. I don't know if she is happy or sad or confused, and I want to ask her what I can do, but when I feel her squeeze me harder, I realize that I am doing everything I can for her in this moment.

---

AS WE LIE ON OUR BACKS, LOOKING UP AT THE ceiling, the sounds of Jill Scott filling the space around us, I say, "We only have three days left."

"I know," she says, her voice full of doubtful exasperation.

"We should be together."

She says nothing. She only lies next to me, her eyes still focused on the blue tint of darkness on my ceiling.

I wish I knew what she was thinking, but I can't read her words or her actions at this point. "You know I meant what I said earlier," I finally say.

"Yes," she responds. "I know."

"Did you mean what you said?"

She half-chuckles in an odd sarcastic way. "You already know the deal, Chucky."

"Maybe I do; maybe I don't. Every time I want to believe this detached persona you project you open yourself even more to me. I don't know what to make of this. Sometimes I think you are falling in love with me, and other times I think you want to tell me to leave you alone. But the thing is that you don't. You keep coming back, and now I'm caught up in these feelings I have for you."

"What do you want me to do?" she says.

"Follow your heart."

She turns to face me. "What if my heart doesn't know?"

I want to say some smooth shit that would convince her that I am the best choice for her, but the words fail me.

"Can you hold me?" she asks, her eyes almost pleading with me.

I take her in my arms, and she immediately nestles herself against me, where we remain until we both give way to the fatigue coursing through our bodies.

WHEN I WAKE AROUND 5:30 A.M., SHE IS GONE.

During the time we spent together, I had wondered how it would happen, how she would call it quits. Would it be a dinner conversation? Would we still be lying in orgasmic bliss when she arose from the bed to dress? Would it be a text message or a phone call? But nothing could have prepared me to awake in my bed to find myself alone, hours after we told each other, "I love you."

The emptiness of my bed is amplified even more by the fact that the blue light is still on, the music playing softly in the background. I walk throughout my apartment, looking for any trace of her. There is no overnight bag, not so much as a bobby pin, and even more, there is no note. There is just this coolness that causes my body to shiver. I look out my window and her car is gone.

I return to my room and pick up my phone from the speaker cradle. As I wait for her to answer her phone, the voicemail comes on, so I call again. The same thing.

Sitting on my bed, my head resting in my hands, I watch the rising of the sun through my bedroom blinds.

So this is how it ends. In the words of Junot Díaz's character Yunior, I realize that this is how I will lose her—and there are no words for how much it hurts.

## 8

## NO RHYME OR REASON

The hardest reality to face once you have fallen in love with someone is that you were the other guy. I was only there for a limited time to fill a void. This situation is not so uncommon, and there are even other people out there who thrive in these scenarios.

I wish I were one of them.

My mind races through the list of songs that songwriters have articulated on this subject so well throughout the years.

*"Everything I Miss At Home" - Cherrelle*

*"No Rhyme, No Reason" - George Duke*

*"Secret Lovers" - Atlantic Starr*

*"As We Lay" - Shirley Murdock*

And the list goes on and on with songs on the other side of the 1980s. These songs do well because there is a need for them. I feel as though I could write a few of them right now myself. The only thing that I imagine would be worse than what I'm feeling is if I were her boyfriend and she was experiencing all of this with some other guy.

I try her on her cell phone again later in the day,

and when she doesn't answer, I realize I have no one to blame but myself.

———

I MET MAYA SMITH BECAUSE SHE USED TO WORK AT A diner I frequented back when I was living in my grandmother's basement. I was a long way from my current weight, and my self-esteem needed a bit of work, but she was kind to me and that went a long way.

I would order the weekly Salisbury steak special with mashed potatoes, and she was always my server. Then one day while I was using the restroom at the restaurant I overhead someone robbing the restaurant through the restroom door. I was so worried about what could have happened to Maya that I burst through the door and just happened to slam the door into the dude holding up the joint. He dropped his gun, and I threw myself on top of him until the police came.

It was the only time in my life where I ever felt like a hero, but even that meant little to me, especially when compared to the fact that Maya was now interested in me. As any person who has seen the movie *Speed* already knows, relationships built around intense action fail to hold up over time. Maya and I were no exception.

Marcia, on the other hand, is the first woman who was ever drawn to me without the need for some dynamic outside factor. That made this experience feel very different. I wasn't a hero; I was just a guy she was drawn to for whatever reason a woman can be drawn to a man, and she was a woman I was drawn to, although I would have, at any other time, have viewed her as being outside my league.

I look at my cell phone, hoping to see any message from her. I even go so far as to troll her Twitter account, just to make sure she's actually alive (she is). And even though I know she has forty-eight hours left on her Rumspringa, I know in my heart that we're over.

I consider calling J or Ran, but I'm afraid I will get an "I told you so." I also think about calling Cool or Dizzy, but I know that they are both in love with women who are in love with them and talking with them would only depress me further.

I feel so down and out that I could kick sixteen bars on Pharcyde's "Passing Me By," a song where all of the members of the group lament their bad luck with their love interests. I think about that last verse where dude sends the girl a love letter that comes back three days later "Return to Sender." If my memory serves me correctly, Dizzy wrote a letter for Lailah when they were on the verge of ending their engagement. If I thought it would help, I'd do the same.

My only hope is that Marcia will contact me once she and her boyfriend have reconnected after the Rumspringa. But how likely is that? They have fifteen years of something. The question is will that fifteen years of something trump our nearly two weeks and the promise of a future built on those weeks?

When I lie down on my bed and close my eyes, I replay each moment we spent together. I see her smiling, laughing at my jokes, watching movies with me, eating with me, and playing Jeopardy with me as we tag team while watching the TV show. But those moments when we were intimate burn the freshest in my memory, and that alone makes me feel some optimism about our future.

Still, I have not heard from her all day, and if tomorrow is the same as today, I doubt that optimism will remain.

———

THE RUMSPRINGA HAS OFFICIALLY ENDED, bookending the most amazing moment in my life between two invisible, seemingly arbitrary, boundaries that I had no role in erecting.

The only equivalent I can think of for what I have experienced is having been dumped. Granted, that would not be a first for me. Maya left me. But this feels *different*.

I wasn't in love with Maya. Even now, it's hard for me to admit I'm in love with Marcia, especially given the length of time we spent with each other, but sometimes your heart is oblivious to the calendar. I read somewhere that often times the short relationships are the most intense, and based upon this experience, I have little choice but to agree.

How a person knows that he loves someone is a peculiar thing anyway. I imagine for many guys it is not that different from my situation. Some people you love and others you don't. It isn't a meritocracy thing where a woman has to earn a man's love with loyalty or pampering. It's just something a man knows. That's the reason why I was afraid of Marcia initially—not that I loved her then, but I knew she was a person who could potentially bring that out of me.

I wonder if her boyfriend, Von, felt that way about her fifteen years ago. My guess is that he didn't, or he wouldn't have gone along with this Rumspringa thing.

When I try to think about this situation from Marcia's perspective, I can only see one thing: time in a relationship is an investment, and this much time has to pay off some kind of way. That's the only way I can wrap my mind around the fact that she hasn't left him for me. She is protecting her investment. The funny thing is that men don't tend to think that way at all. So while there is a part of me that hopes that she gets what she wants (because you want that for people you love), there's another part of me that doesn't want her to get what she wants. I *almost* feel guilty about that.

I look at my phone and consider attempting one last call, not remotely concerned about how thirsty I might appear, but I decide against it. Instead, I check her Facebook page.

According to her profile, she uploaded a new photo today, and it's one of her and Von. As I look at this dude, I scratch my head at what has attracted her to him. He is a really tall, light complexioned guy with a nose that looks like it's been broken a few times. His eyes look like they are bulging from their sockets, and he has a scraggly, unkempt beard. She is standing next to him, wearing that sweet smile that I have come to think of as *my* smile. Beneath the photo is the comment "I said, 'Yes!'" That's when I examine the picture more closely.

*Is that what I think it is? A fucking ring? Seriously?*

I stare at that picture for a few minutes, my body a hollow shell of where passion once resided. I need more than ever to talk to her.

I send her a quick direct message to her inbox. There are only two words: *What happened?*

## 9

## ALL'S WELL

It takes Marcia nearly two weeks to respond to my Facebook message, and her response leaves too much to be desired:

*When he came back, he told me that this experience taught him how much he loved me and couldn't be without me. He proposed to me on that first night. I can't afford to look back now. He is my future. I didn't mean to hurt you. I hope that you find the kind of happiness that you so richly deserve.*

I stare at the message, incredulous. I wonder for a moment if an engagement ring could so easily cause a woman's brain to be hijacked. Everything that we did and experienced would suggest that there was no way she could go through with any of this. If I were a betting man, after that first week of our being together, I would have easily gone all-in.

How could she have given so much of herself to me in such a short period of time for it not to mean anything? We were lovers on every level. There is absolutely no logic in any of this, but when it comes to emotions, I'm guessing there rarely are.

"You should listen to the song 'Reasons' by Earth, Wind & Fire. It might put some of this stuff into perspective," Ran says.

"Isn't that a love song?"

"It sounds like one if you're not paying attention. Think about it, dude. 'We're in the wrong place to be real.' There's not a happy ending to that song, but Philip Bailey sings the hell out of it in a way that makes you think the opposite. I once heard him say that people would have that song performed at their weddings. Even he had to shake his head on that one."

I sigh. "If I listen to that song, I'd probably be even more depressed than I am now."

Ran scoots his office chair closer to mine and leans in, so as to not be heard, and says, "You know I'm your boy, right?"

"Yeah, I know."

"Well, consider this: you've been reeling from her being gone longer than you were actually with her. You think it might be time to move on?"

I shake my head. "I just don't get it."

"See, one of the things about brothers like you is that you're too logical. You think that things have to make sense, that motivations have to be understood. I mean, don't get it twisted. There's definitely a merit to that with some things, but love is an emotion and many women are guided by emotions, not necessarily logic."

"But isn't that sexist?" I say.

"I don't really think it is. I'm not talking about all people of any gender, but to ignore the psychological differences between the sexes could result in serious misunderstandings, your situation for example."

"I think I liked your Earth, Wind & Fire recommendation better."

Ran nods. "Yeah. People tend to associate me with musical references."

*No shit, Sherlock.*

I look at the clock on the wall across the room. It reads 4:55 p.m.

"So what do you have planned for tonight?" I ask.

"Dinner with the family. Maybe we'll go catch a movie."

"Well, give my best to Lauren and Zoë."

"Will do," he responds. "And Chuck?"

"Yeah?"

"Chin up, dude. Life goes on. There's something much better for you waiting around the corner."

"From your mouth to God's ears," I respond.

He smiles and nods, then packs up his bag, pats me on the shoulder, and walks away.

I turn to my desktop and start shutting it down. I have no plans for the evening, and I am in no hurry, so I take my time organizing the paperwork on my desk so I can get off to a clean start tomorrow morning.

It feels like Dizzy and Lailah got married a long time ago and that my relationship (if you could call it that) was during another lifetime. In the weeks since Marcia left, I have lost interest in following her on social media or attempting to call her. For me to continue snooping around would only confirm that I have in fact turned into a creepy guy. I refuse to go there.

I pack up my backpack and head for the exit door. As I walk past one of the cubicles on the way to the door, though, I see a picture of Princess Leia in her Jabba the Hut slave costume posted to the wall of someone's cubicle. My mind immediately goes back to Marcia, and I see her standing there in that small motel room in Daily, Mississippi, modeling her bra and panties set for me. I smile.

By the time I step out the front door and onto the street, traffic around Euclid and Moreland is pretty thick. I know if I hop in my car right now and start trying to drive home I will get stuck in traffic, so I walk around the corner, just off of Moreland, and have a seat on one of the benches. I pull out my headphones, plug them into my phone, and pull up some Robert Glasper on iTunes.

I watch people walk by and wonder where they're headed. Are they headed to meet loved ones or discover new ones? That's always the question when you see people coming and going: *Where?* It's a simple question, but the answer can tell a person so much. The fact that I am headed home to my apartment says something about me. The funny thing is that I have been doing this very thing ever since I moved out of my grandmother's basement, but only in these past few weeks has doing this felt like a lonely activity. Missing someone can totally transform how everyday things appear.

Once several songs have played, I take off my headphones and place them back in my backpack. As I stand to leave, I feel a hand press on my shoulder, and I jump instinctively.

"Chucky," I hear her say, and for a moment, I consider not turning around.

When I finally turn around and see Marcia's face, I am not sure I want to hear anything she has to say.

I look at her, but I don't say anything. In all of the time I had been replaying the possibility of something like this happening, I never considered the possibility that I would feel anything less than happiness from seeing her face. As I look at her now, all I can think is that she chose him, not me.

"Chucky, can we talk?"

I nod and slide over on the bench.

She sits down next to me. It takes me a second to see that she is not wearing that ring from the Facebook photo.

"Let me start off by saying that I'm sorry," she says.

"Sorry for what?" I say sarcastically.

"So it's going to be that type of conversation?"

"I'm just saying. There's so much that I don't know about all of this, so you'll have to be a little more specific," I respond.

"Fair enough," she says, chuckling nervously under her breath. "I thought a long time about whether or not I should even come down here and put myself out there like this."

"Putting yourself out there? What do you mean? Is it over with Von?"

She places her hands together and nods her head, looking away from me.

"What happened?" I ask.

"Do you really need to know the details?"

"Nope. But I'd still like to hear them."

She laughs. "I can't just tell you that it didn't work?"

"Let me ask you this: if the tables were turned, would you feel comfortable with that answer?"

"I see what you mean," she says. She looks down at her hands for a moment, collecting her thoughts. "Well, he kept sneaking around trying to see several women he had met over the break, and when I called him on it everything went to shit. I gave him back his ring. It's over."

*Serves you right*, I think. Instead, I hold my tongue.

"So do you need my blessing or something?" I say.

"Why? What do you mean?"

"Marcia, why are you here?"

She looks shocked by my question, and I can tell that she never really considered the fact that I would not fall readily into her arms. Now there is an awkward space between us.

When she finally speaks, her voice is soft, weak. "I was hoping that maybe we could start over."

"Answer me this: if he hadn't cheated on you, would you have come back to me?"

Her shoulders rise and fall as she inhales and exhales. "I don't know. Probably not."

"Probably not?" I repeat incredulously. "How do you think that makes me feel?"

"Hurt, maybe."

I look away for a moment, unable to face her.

"That's not a bad thing, though, Chucky. I'm a loyal person when I'm in a relationship. I am always a ride or die woman. When you and I were together, I was committed to only you, but when the Rumspringa ended, I had to be loyal to my boyfriend. If you were my man, I would have been loyal to you, too."

As I listen to her, I reabsorb just how strange this situation was to begin with. She gave me much more than she had planned to give, and I was happy taking that. But when she went back to her boyfriend, I could only deal with my hurt feelings, never really trying to understand how she could leave me. I had assumed it was easy for her to do, not that it was necessary for her to do.

"How do I know you wouldn't leave me for this dude?" I ask.

"Chucky, never in my life have I felt as conflicted about someone as I have you. If I had had my way, I would have only been with you."

"I guess what I'm trying to understand is this: do you want to be with me for loyalty's sake, or do you want to be with me because of love?"

She smiles. "That's easy. It's because I love you. And, as you already know, I'm not obligated to say or feel that."

"That's it," I say. "I don't want you to suffer through a relationship with me simply out of obligation. If you believe in what we have, that's good enough for me."

She nods her head, absorbing this. "I feel you."

"So you're saying that you really want to be with me?"

"Yes. What about you?"

I stand and reach for her hand. In that moment I want to tell her yes, but the word gets stuck on my tongue, and as I swallow, it ebbs back down my throat, trapping itself my chest. I don't know what to think as I stare at her.

I can feel my heart thumping in my chest, the bruise from these past few weeks still throbbing. Her eyes slowly widen from my silence, and she starts to withdraw her hand.

"Come here," I say, taking her in my arms and holding her. She melts against my chest. "Let's get out of here."

~ fin ~

# PORTRAIT OF VENUS

## BONUS STORY

Originally published in
*Lyrotica: An Anthology of Erotic Poetry & Prose*,
edited by Rebecca Ammon

K imberly stared at the mask, fingering the delicate cream-colored plastic. "What is this supposed to be? Some *Lone Ranger* meets *Phantom of the Opera* kind of thing?"

She pulled the string around the back of her head and rested the mask carefully against her face. I smiled, silently applauding myself for selecting something that so evenly complemented the bronze complexion of her skin.

"I appreciate your doing this for me," I said, lifting the DSLR camera from the table positioned against the wall of my basement.

"You just better make me look good. Like Josephine Baker or Pam Grier."

Everything had come together so quickly that I was operating off of a combination of butterflies and adrenaline. The camera was my birthday gift from three weeks ago, the mask just one of several souvenirs I picked up in New Orleans while strolling Royal Street in the French Quarters. I had wanted to shoot nudes in the tradition of Herb Ritts and Marc Baptiste, and while it was much easier to come by the camera, it was next to impossible to come by the model. That was until my friend Kimberly agreed to help me out.

The fact that she had even volunteered was still a bit of a mystery to me. I had known her nearly all of my life, and in that time, she had never shown any interest in serving as a muse to any of my creative endeavors. Once while we were in high school I had made my move only to be shut down. "You're my friend, and I need you to be just that," she told me right before she started dating the captain of the basketball team. Even now that we were still close friends, I was no more a part of her romantic radar than I had been years ago. This was illustrated boldly by the fact that she currently had a boyfriend, some fancy lawyer who practiced international law downtown.

As I prepared my basement, I found myself staring at the thin aqua colored bed sheet in front of the wall. It resembled rippling water as the triad of key, filler, and backlights reflected off the wrinkles in the cloth. Kimberly stood off to the side dressed in a ribbed sleeveless t-shirt, braless, and a pair of loose sweatpants, her feet bare. She had brought a pair of pumps, at my suggestion, and they sat near the wall on the other side of the room.

"Check *you* out," she said when she saw me, camera in hand.

I nodded, trying my best to display the kind of confidence that deep down I was sorely lacking. I was still having trouble realizing that she was actually here. I wanted to ask her why now—after all of this time, but I was afraid to say anything that might turn her mind at the last minute. Maybe she was just being my friend after all. But in a way, it felt like the entire situation was a tease, compounded even more by the fact that her boyfriend would be out of the country for the next few weeks doing work in Jordan. In that window of time I could easily lose myself in Kimberly's eyes a million times—not that she would notice.

She looked over my shoulder. "I love that painting," she said, pointing at the mural of two people intertwined, the bodies melting into one form. I had painted the image in a drunken state one night as I pined over her and why fate had been so cruel as to never allow us to hook up. "It's very sensual," she added.

"Thanks," I responded, trying to suppress the blush burning in my cheeks. I wanted to say more about the mural, but my nerves got the best of me.

I suddenly wondered if I could do Kimberly justice with the photographs. Was I wasting her time? I was just an amateur with a camera well beyond his skill level, yet I was asking her to take off her clothes. I wasn't sure I would have done the same for her had the roles been reversed.

I shot off a few practice shots, just to stall and build up my confidence, before turning to her. "OK. Let's get you beneath the lights over there."

She walked over to the sheet and stood there, barefoot and clothed, while I checked the lighting levels. I hooked up the camera to my laptop and shot a few pictures of her, checking each of them on the display. As far as I could tell, they looked nice.

For the first time since Kimberly arrived, I began to feel the shoot might go well after all and we might just end up with some nice pictures.

"You ready?" I asked, lowering the camera to my side.

"Sure. You got any music or anything. It's kind of quiet in here."

"Hold on," I said, walking over to my laptop. I put on Michael Jackson's "Lady in My Life" and set it to repeat.

Kimberly walked over by the wall and began to lift her shirt above her stomach. She pulled the t-shirt over her breasts, attempting to cover her nipples with her left arm. Carefully, she continued lifting the shirt over her head so as to not remove the mask, no easy task with one arm. As she leaned over to pull down her sweatpants and panties, I was blown away at how exponential her sexiness grew with the increase of her exposed flesh. Just beneath her navel was a tattoo of the word "love" in cursive, small and suggestive.

"You look amazing," I said, as she stood before me completely nude, her left arm still crossing her chest. "It's OK if you want to put your arm down."

She blushed. "I guess I'm trying to build up the courage for you to see me like this."

She was already naked, and I could see the flatness of her stomach, the curviness of her hips, and even the low trim of the hair that rested in the sweet spot where her legs met. Still, her hand was guarding what remained of her. I placed the camera on the table and walked over to her. Resting my hand gently on the warm flesh of her shoulder, I said, "It's OK. We don't have to do anything that you're uncomfortable with. In fact, I like that pose. Do you mind walking over here and letting me get a shot of you like that?"

"Really? I feel so silly."

"Trust me. You look fine."

Kimberly stepped over and allowed me to position her against the backdrop. I had her turn her body to me at an angle, her arm still crossing her chest.

"I'm going to shoot from the waist up on this one. OK?"

"OK."

I snapped a few shots, centered and off-centered, alternating my focus between her and the background behind her, changing angles every few shots. I glanced again at my laptop to check out the composition of my shots. That's when I noticed that Kimberly's arm had fallen during the last few shots. She was now standing completely naked before me, and I hadn't even noticed.

I looked up from my laptop, taking in the round, firm shape of her breasts and the way her nipples seemed to swell in the coolness of the room. "You are perfect."

She lifted her hand to her mouth to keep from laughing aloud. "Yeah, right."

"I'm serious, Kim. I wish you could see yourself through my eyes."

"Well, can I see the pictures?"

"Not yet," I said, refocusing my lens on her. "I want it to be a surprise."

She smiled, placing her hands on her hips. "So how do you want me to pose now?"

While I had originally planned out most of my shots, I surprised myself when I responded, "I'll follow you. Do what you feel."

She rolled her eyes for a moment, trying to suppress a smile. Then she lifted her hands above her masked face like a superhero ballerina and stood on her tiptoes.

I smiled, continuing to snap away.

Her arms extended slowly as she moved her body fluidly with the rhythm of the music. She was now dancing, her body taking on shape after shape. As she extended and stretched her legs and arms, the definition in her muscles formed highlights to her body.

And then something happened. She stared directly into the lens, removing the mask so that she was no longer anonymous. It hung gently around her neck for a moment before she lifted it over her head and tossed it onto the chair situated just off the turquoise sheet.

Up until that moment, she had been in her own space, pretending to be someone else. Now she was looking directly at me, and it was Kimberly, not her masked doppelganger.

She ran her fingers through her curly hair. With her right hand, she blew a kiss toward the camera.

"Nice," I said, my face flush with excitement, but my finger continuing to snap pictures. "Very sexy."

She smiled, sliding a finger into her mouth. She removed it slowly, allowing traces of saliva to mark her down her chest and onto her nipple.

I struggled to hold the camera firmly in my

hands, but the butterflies racing in my stomach teased me, lubricating my palms so that I almost dropped it several times.

She reinserted her finger into her mouth, this time drawing a line to her other nipple. With her thighs pressed together, she bent herself forward ever so slightly and placed her index finger in front of her sealed mouth, a gesture of silence. Then with her other hand, she navigated her way back to her middle, parting her legs again.

My finger continued involuntarily snapping pictures, my mind now paralyzed with longing.

She lowered herself down onto the turquoise sheet, lying sideways from the camera, and arched her back so I could see her pushing her body upward, her ass lifting from the sheet, her hand, glistening with the juices of her own excitement, moving back and forth between her legs. She moaned, pinching her nipple lightly with her other hand, as her feet sought friction against the smoothness of the sheet.

I lowered the camera to my side, half-expecting her to stop now that she was no longer being photographed. She continued moving her body, though, making herself feel good. I could feel myself stiffen as I watched her, her hand floating above her crotch as two fingers moved in small, delicate patterns. She could have been doing this alone in her bedroom for the one thousandth time the way she moved so fluidly.

Kneeling down beside her, I placed the camera on the floor. I leaned over and kissed her forehead. Her skin was warm beneath my lips, and I felt as if I were dissolving into her glow. Her eyes fluttered for a moment, but remained sealed. She continued to moan, as I lifted my lips and placed them gently over hers. Her tongue brushed softly against mine, and with her free hand, she pressed firmly against my chest, rubbing it, her fingernails sending chills throughout my body.

I removed my shirt and took one of her nipples into my mouth, my tongue dancing like a feather against her skin. Her body continued to arch, willing me to kiss her farther down her body and across the soft flesh of her stomach.

When I reached the "love" tattoo that trailed beneath her navel, my tongue traced along each letter, outlining it, as if I could bring the emotion out of her towards me. I could feel her arm brushing lightly against my forehead as she continued pleasuring herself. Gently I moved my mouth down to where her moist flesh and fingers intersected.

Lifting her hand, I finished what she had begun.

We slid back and forth across the sheet as the music played softly around us.

I tasted her. She tasted me.

The skin of our bodies kissed with an aching to be connected into one form.

I entered her. She enveloped me.

We uttered breathless, unintelligible moans into each other's ear, our own language, created from our youth and manifested now in this sweaty embrace.

When we came, it felt as if the sun had exploded between us, leaving our bodies tingling in the coolness of the air. I looked at the ceiling, savoring the feeling of her lips against my neck and the scent of her hair as it brushed the side of my face.

For a while neither of us said anything, as if

speaking would somehow plant our feet back into reality. So I held her close to me, our legs interlocked, wishing that we could stay that way forever.

"The painting on the wall," she started, her voice drifting softly over my body, "that's us, isn't it?"

"Yes."

She nestled her head in the crook of my arm, seemingly content in her silence.

I wanted so badly to ask her, "What now?" but I couldn't bring myself to say anything that would take her out of the moment. Instead, I held her close to me, enjoying the feeling of her body spooned in mine as we drifted off to sleep.

I woke a few hours later, the sky through my window still pitch black. Feeling for Kimberly, I slowly realized that I was alone on that cool sheet. Not even the imprint of her body remained amid the ruffled cloth. An empty feeling hit me hard, and I wondered what had happened. Had she even been here at all? Only the mask lying on the floor against the wall made me hold fast to the fact we had actually made love earlier.

Rising to my feet, I looked for any traces of her: a handwritten note, a strand of hair, anything. Only Michael Jackson's soft, crooning voice remained in the void, cycling on repeat from earlier. Then I remembered: the camera!

I quickly walked over to the DSLR and turned it on. As it booted up, I held my breath. When the display launched, I felt myself tumble down into the pit in my stomach. There were only two pictures on my camera, both of Kimberly from the waist up, disguised in that mask, her arm draped across her breasts. All of the other pictures had been deleted. It was as if nothing had ever happened.

But it did, I was convinced. I could still feel the phantom movements of her body rocking against me as my erection returned. I knew right then that I would have to cling to that sensation before even it, too, disappeared.

# FONDLING MY MUSE

## BONUS STORY

Originally published in
*Succulent: Chocolate Flava 2,*
edited by Zane

T he week ended with my head in a daze, stories circling my brain. I could still feel a slight cramp in my hand from all of the homework assignments I struggled to complete over the course of the week. I had known that the Black Writer's Workshop would be exhausting when I applied several months ago. Like many others in attendance, I had felt the need to do something affirmative to prove to myself that I was in fact taking myself seriously as a writer. This was my chance to be around people and call myself a writer without being ridiculed. I wasn't a computer programmer anymore. I was just someone who was working on his short stories, aiming at getting a book completed by the end of the year. So when I packed up my things for a week in New York, I had no idea that I would meet her, the muse who would get me through the week.

I first saw her during the opening dinner meet-

and-greet. She didn't really stand out very much either. She had a kind of funky Afro, kind of like Nbushe Wright's doo in *Dead Presidents*. Her Stevie Wonder t-shirt hung lazily from her body, and if it had not been for her shorts riding up those long, sculpted legs, it might've taken me a little longer to really notice her. She had a casual beauty like Sanaa Lathan, the kind of beauty that was subtle in drawing attention. I had always found that type of woman irresistible.

After introducing myself and learning that her name was Meredith, I began to keep an eye out for her during our workshop breaks and during the meals we ate at the university cafeteria. On the second day, while having lunch, I spotted her at a table with several of her classmates.

"Excuse me," I said, as I approached. "Do you mind if I sit here?"

She looked up at me and smiled. "No. It's cool."

I sat down diagonally from her, introducing myself to the two other women seated nearby. Being the only man at the table, the women quickly directed their attention toward me.

"So where are you from?" the woman named Rachelle asked.

"Mississippi," I responded.

"Ooh, you probably had to escape slavery to get here," said the one named Diamond.

"And I ain't never goin' back. Nah, sur. I's likes my freedom!"

They laughed, but I hardly noticed anyone, except Meredith. She had a sexiness that danced just beneath the surface, and at that moment, all I wanted to do was undress her, lay her down on her stomach and plant kisses all along her chocolate moon-shaped ass.

"You here for poetry or fiction?" Meredith asked.

"Fiction."

"Really? Me too. Whose your workshop teacher?"

"Jonathan Cadet."

"Man, I was trying to get him for my class. I'm taking Cynthia Wordley. She's great though."

"Well, I'd love to read some of your stuff sometime," I said.

"I don't know," she said. "Like Erykah Badu says, 'I'm an artist, and I sensitive about my shit!'"

Her smile made me smile, and from then on, I found myself mysteriously sliding into this groove, writing the same kinds of stories all week long for my workshop. The first story was about a man and a woman who met at a sex anonymous meeting and fell off the wagon soon afterwards. The second story was about a guy having repeated wet dreams about the same woman every night. The third story was about a woman who caught a man jacking off at a stoplight late one night and offered to finish the job for him. It had gotten to the point that when I came to class Mr. Cadet would have an assuming smirk on his face. One day he flat-out asked me if there was something thematic that I was trying to accomplish with my randy collection of stories.

"I don't know. I think I'm just following where my muse leads."

He nodded. "Well, it's good to have a muse. Stirs the creative juices."

Creative juices? I wanted to swim in those.

But I was a little too nervous to really step up and put it out there with Meredith, so I laid low and chatted with her during the brief moments when we'd connect during the day. Nothing special. Just enough to keep my imagination sparked. Before I knew it, the last day of the workshop had arrived, and the realization that I would probably never see her again began to sink in. I had written all of these stories about being with her, all of these *fantasies*, and it was about to be over. Just like that.

Another realization dawned on me too: I had spent the entire week writing out my sexual frustrations with stories that I would probably never be able to use professionally, not unless Zane found one of them worthy of publishing in an anthology. If I didn't put it out there with Meredith, then I would have wasted a week.

That night I didn't see her at the banquet, and when a group of my classmates had decided to go out for drinks, I kept an eye out for her, hoping our paths would cross going in and out of pubs. When I didn't see her out and about or hanging out in front of the dorm with other students, I began to question whether she had already left, headed home. When the thought that I had completely blown it set in, I promised myself that if I should see her before the program officially ended the following morning, then I would put it all on the line.

I knew that she was staying in a room at the end of the hall on the floor above mine, so in a final attempt to contact her, I went up to her dorm room a few minutes before eleven that night and knocked on the door. I could hear shuffling as the door opened slowly.

"Yeah," she whispered, squinting her eyes against

the light of the hallway. It was pitch black in her room.

"Just wanted to see you before you dipped out tomorrow."

"Oh, OK," she said, barely coherent. "How are you doing?"

"I'm good," I said. "And you?"

"Just tired. I gotta catch a flight at eight in the morning, so I have to get up at the ass-crack of dawn."

"Oh," I said, chuckling at her joke.

She would be at the airport in a few hours, and I wanted to kick myself for not coming by her room earlier or even trying to get at her before the last day. I could have just wished her well with her writing, but I knew that if I didn't tell her how I felt, I would never get the opportunity to. The words came out in a blur.

"Meredith, I know that this is really bad timing, but I just had to let you know that I've been feeling you all week. I can't stop thinking about you. Hell, all of the stories I wrote this week were about you."

She looked at me for a moment as if I had told her that Malcolm X was really a Baptist preacher.

I continued. "I hate that it took me this long to tell you, but I couldn't let you leave without knowing that I am really attracted to you, your voice, your smile, your personality. On that first day when I saw you, something in me wanted to connect with you."

The more I listened to myself, the cornier the stuff I was saying sounded. I was messing up big time, but at least I was getting the basic idea out there. She had an expression on her face like "this nigga is crazy," and I couldn't blame her.

"Well. That's all. I was hoping to talk with you a little bit before you left, but I didn't want to cut into your sleep. I guess I should lay it down myself."

She nodded her head.

As I started to walk away, she said, "You wrote stories about me?"

"Yes," I said, turning around.

"Well, were they any good?"

"I don't know if they were, but it felt good writing them."

She smiled as she closed the door.

---

A HALF HOUR LATER, I WAS LYING ON TOP OF THE covers on my bed listening to Raheem DeVaughn on the portable boom box I had sitting on the desk in my room. Although the lights were out, I could still catch a mild glow of light through the blinds, reminding me that the city was right outside my window. I had been staring at the ceiling so long, lost in my thoughts, that I had assumed I was asleep.

The knock was very soft, but somehow I still heard it. Dressed in only my boxers and a t-shirt, I got up and walked to the door. Looking through the peephole, I could see Meredith standing there in an oversized Clark Atlanta sweatshirt, her flannel pajama bottoms hanging down over her New Balance running shoes. I opened the door, and my stomach immediately started to churn with butterflies.

"Come in," I offered. I cleared off a spot on my bed for her to sit down.

It took everything I had in me to suppress my smile. She had actually come to my room! It didn't matter what for either. She was there, and that was really all that mattered.

"Hey, Marlon, I just wanted to take a look at some of your stories. I don't think any guy has ever written a story about me before. I just had to see what you had to say."

"No problem," I said, pulling out the stack of stories I had printed out during the week. I had arranged them in the sequence in which they were written, so the sex-aholic meeting one was on the top. I handed them to her before I realized that I should be embarrassed by how blatant my stories were. Meredith had really brought out the freak in me.

As I sat in the chair by my desk, facing my bed, I watched her read the first story. She nodded occasionally, as if to say, "Interesting." When she finished the first story, she placed it back on the stack resting next to her on the bed.

"So *I* inspired you to write a story about two sex addicts?"

"Well, sort of. More like motivation."

"Motivation? Are all of the stories like this?"

Now I was really embarrassed. "More or less."

She lowered her head for a moment as if to reflect over what she had just read. Lifting her head, she slid out of my bed and stood up in front of me. "I am Meredith Jones, and I—" she sighed, in a voice of mock frustration, "—am addicted to sex."

I looked at her with my eyebrow raised, and just then I saw her smile, that same smile from the first day I had lunch with her. I stood up from my seat.

"I am Marlon Shepherd, and I *too* am addicted to sex."

The words were nearly identical to the words in the story, save our names. I could feel my erection starting to push the fabric of my boxers.

"So, Marlon, what do we do now," she said, looking down at my erection.

Her mouth sealed around mine before I could catch my thoughts, and her tongue danced against mine, causing me to ease my hands slowly down her back, around her waist, and onto her ass. She moaned as we fell back onto the bed.

I lifted her sweatshirt and smiled when I realized that she wasn't wearing a bra. I held one of her breasts in my hand and flicked my tongue across her nipple, quickly enveloping it with the warmth of my mouth. My hand eased down into her flannel pajama bottoms, and at that moment, I realized that she had only been wearing the sweatshirt, pajama bottoms, and sneakers—nothing beneath!

Slowly I went over the length of her body massaging her muscles with my fingertips and replacing the sensation with my mouth. I made a soft wet trail from her neck, down below her navel, and as my lips reached the inner part of her hip, I lifted her legs to drape over my shoulders. She eased toward me, allowing her clit to rub against the tip of my nose before sliding down onto my tongue. She rocked into me as I licked and sucked, her hands holding my head as she moved her body back and forth. I cupped my hands beneath her ass, lifting her into me, and her legs shot out, erect, as she screamed out in ecstasy, shivering.

I stood back from the bed, admiring her sexy

body reclined in the light of the room, her wetness dripping down onto my sheets. She slowly sat up on the edge of my bed and slid one hand up my t-shirt onto my chest, as she pulled my throbbing erection from my boxers with her other hand and ran her tongue along the entire length of my shaft. I moved my hips forward involuntarily, as she took the head into her mouth. Working me back and forth with her hands, I did everything I could to keep from cumming. I wanted to feel her sliding up and down me before I came.

Wetting up my shaft with her saliva, she guided me between her legs and eased me into her hot wetness. The warmth worked its way down my shaft as I wrapped myself completely around her. Her hands rubbed my back, and I stroked her as if it were the last thing I would ever do in life. Lifting her legs into a "V" formation, I eased myself into her until she gasped. As I rotated my hips, I looked down at her beautiful, sexy chocolate complexion; her full, firm breasts; and her athletic body. I massaged her calves with my fingertips as I held her legs spread.

"Ooh, I like it!" she cooed. "It feels so good!"

I smiled, but I couldn't respond because she felt so incredible that I could cum if she so much as wiggled a toe. I wanted to hold off and enjoy her all night. I didn't want her to get on that plane the next morning and leave without knowing that she was all that.

We rolled over, and she climbed on top of me, sliding her hips into mine. I could feel her wetness dripping down my balls as she pushed into me and wiggled her body. And when she was ready, she did a Kegel pull that made me scream out.

"Oh, shit! I'm gonna cum!"

She pulled me into her as I felt myself exploding in what felt like a psychedelic Technicolor orgasm, my erection throbbing in repetition as her walls tightened around me. We held on to each other for what seemed like one interminable moment before realizing how late it was.

As she dressed, I watched her cover up her perfection with each piece of clothing I had taken off earlier.

"I want a copy of the stories," she said.

"Take them. I have the files on my laptop."

I walked her to the door and kissed her. "Sleep well," she whispered, caressing my face.

I offered to walk her back to her room, but she refused, saying that she was fine. She only asked me to do one thing for her just before she left: she asked me to write this story.

*B-Sides and Remixes*

*30 Love: A Novel*

*Mojo's Guitar: A Novel/(Il était une fois Morris Jones)*

*Afro Nerd in Love: A Novella*

*The Keys of My Soul: A Novel*

*The Race of Races: A Novel*

*The Illest: A Novella*

*Bessie, Bop, or Bach: Collected Stories*

*Four Floors (with Sabin Prentis)*

*Black Hand Side: Stories*

*White Pages: A Novel*

*She Lives in My Lap*

*Reverb*

*Work-In-Progress*

*Daykeeper*

*Most of My Heroes Don't Appear On No Stamps*

*Portable Black Magic*

Ran Walker is the winner of the 2019 National Indie Author of the Year Award (selected by judges from Library Journal, Publisher's Weekly, IngramSpark, St. Martin's Press, and Writer's Digest), the 2019 Black Caucus of the American Library Association Best Fiction Ebook Award, and the 2018 Virginia Indie Author Project Award for Adult Fiction. He is also the recipient of both a 2005 Mississippi Arts Commission/NEA artist grant and a 2006 artist mini-grant. He served as an Artist-in-Residence with the Mississippi Arts Commission in 2006. Additionally, he is a past participant in the Hurston-Wright Writers Week Workshop and is the recipient of a fellowship from the Callaloo Writers Workshop. He teaches creative writing at Hampton University and lives in Virginia with his wife and daughter.

www.ingramcontent.com/pod-product-compliance
Lightning Source LLC
Chambersburg PA
CBHW070312120726
47910CB00007B/2456